Day Leclaire invites you to a wedding...

The Location: The Cinderella Ball.

The Bride: Nikki Ashton—young, single. Well, technically single, and that's the problem. Her boss, her colleagues all think she's happily married—now all she needs is the man to prove it!

The Groom: Jonah Alexander has come to the ball to stop a wedding, not start one. But accidents do happen, and somehow or other he's ended up with Nikki as his *Accidental Wife!*

And it could be your own!

On one very special night, single people from all over America come together in the hope of finding that special ingredient for a happy-ever-after—their soulmate. The Cinderella Ball offers the opportunity for immediate matrimony: come single, leave wed. Which is exactly what is about to happen to three unsuspecting couples in Day Leclaire's magical new trilogy:

Titles in this series are:

November: TEMPORARY
December: ACCIDENTAL WIFE
January 1997: SHOTGUN MARRIAGE

Dear Reader,

I just love Christmas! I love the renewed spirit of love and community, of faith and happiness. But most of all, I love being with my family. Okay, I'll be honest. There are times when families can be exasperating, not to mention nosy and interfering. But I wouldn't trade a single second of my time with any of them. Those moments are infinitely precious and gone all too soon.

I guess that's how Nikki and Jonah's story evolved. They're two people who'd go to any lengths to keep their families happy—even attend the Cinderella Ball and marry a total stranger.

So, amidst the hustle and bustle of this holiday season, take a moment and sneak away for a few hours of romance. Join Nikki, an independent, career-minded redhead, and Jonah, the family "fix-it" man, as they find love one very special Christmas.

And have a joyous holiday season!

Love,

Day Leclaire

Day Leclaire
Accidental Wife

Harlequin Books

TORONTO • NEW YORK • LONDON
AMSTERDAM • PARIS • SYDNEY • HAMBURG
STOCKHOLM • ATHENS • TOKYO • MILAN
MADRID • WARSAW • BUDAPEST • AUCKLAND

To Frank, Donna and Keli Totton.
Your love and support mean the world to me.
And special thanks to Dorothy Smith for explaining the
ins and outs of getting married Nevada-style.

ISBN 0-373-03438-5

ACCIDENTAL WIFE

First North American Publication 1996.

PROLOGUE

Park Slope in Brooklyn, New York

NIKKI leaned back against the wall and closed her eyes, fighting for control. Her sister's voice continued—relentless and sincere, inflicting wounds as painful as they were unintentional.

"I'm sorry," Krista repeated. "I don't know why you bothered to phone when you already know my answer. I can't. I owe Nikki. I won't desert her now."

Why hadn't she realized? Nikki wondered in anguish. Why hadn't she noticed that Krista's needs were no longer the same as seven years ago?

"She's my sister, that's why!" Krista's voice rose in anger. "She gave up everything to take care of me. What do you want me to say? Thanks. You saved my life but now I'm out of here? I've decided to move in with my girlfriend?"

Saved her life? Nikki shook her head. She'd done so little. Offering a home when Krista's husband had died had seemed the only logical option. She'd been pregnant. What other choice was there? Family came first. Family always came first.

"Well, I can't and that's the end of it! After all she's sacrificed for me, the least I can do is be there for her now. Keli and I are all she has. And we're staying until she doesn't need us anymore."

Nikki didn't wait to hear the rest of the conversation. Silently, she retraced her steps down the hallway and entered the small room she used as a secondary office. Crossing to the desk, she opened the top drawer and

5

removed a thick, gold-embossed envelope. It weighted her hand like a lump of lead, and yet the elegant ticket inside was anything but. An engraved wafer of gold metal, it offered a solution to all her problems.

She had prayed she wouldn't need to resort to such a drastic alternative. A choked laugh escaped before she could prevent it. She'd purchased the ticket because the situation at work had grown so untenable. It had never occurred to her that she'd have a dual reason for going ahead with her plan. Unfortunately, overhearing Krista's conversation had closed all avenues but one.

Slowly, she withdrew a white velvet pouch from the envelope. Inside the protective casing, the ticket shimmered as though alive, flooding the room with a brilliant, golden promise. For many people, the ticket would represent a dream come true.

Before she could control it, a lone tear slid down her cheek.

So why did it feel like a nightmare?

Chicago, Illinois

"Oh, Jonah, thank heaven you came." Della Sanders flew into her son's arms and hugged him fiercely.

A hint of amusement lightened Jonah Alexander's grim expression. "Did you doubt I would?" he responded, wrapping his mother in a gentle embrace.

She was a tiny creature, brimming with passion and energy and emotion. She was also a woman who inspired unwavering devotion. Jonah had spent a lifetime watching as she charmed those around her with unconscious ease. Some singular quality reflected in her soft hazel eyes and shy, welcoming smile could win over even the most hardened cases. And in her second husband's line of work, hardened cases were the rule rather than the exception. Hell, she'd won over Loren Sanders—a steely, confirmed bachelor—in five seconds flat.

Della peeked over her shoulder at her husband and offered an apologetic smile. "Loren wasn't certain you'd be willing to bail Eric out of this latest mess." Her breath escaped in an exasperated sigh. "And to be perfectly honest, I wasn't, either. He's really gotten himself into a pickle this time."

Reaching around his mother, Jonah offered a hand to his stepfather. "You shouldn't have waited before getting in touch, Loren. Family always comes first with me. You know that."

It had ever since Jonah had been a tough, angry ten-year-old who'd unexpectedly found himself graced with a stepfather who'd appealed to both his intellect as well as his emotions. Loren had become an unconditional friend. And the deep and enduring love he'd given Della for the past twenty-five years sealed Jonah's eternal support and gratitude.

"You've always been a good brother to Eric," Loren said. "But the European operation keeps you so busy, we hated to bother you with this. Besides, we didn't realize how serious it was until recently. I just hope we're not too late."

Jonah released his mother and crossed to the floor-to-ceiling windows. The Sanderses' Chicago condominium commanded a stunning view of Lake Michigan—a view that under normal circumstances he'd have taken the time to appreciate. "Tell me about it," he requested, turning his back on the expanse of tinted glass.

"Eric's fallen for a married woman," Della announced starkly. "An *older* married woman."

Jonah lifted an eyebrow. Not the smartest thing Eric had ever done, but hardly the most reprehensible. "And?"

"And she works for us," Loren explained. "This ... relationship is interfering with both her performance and his. Between them they almost lost the Dearfield account."

Jonah swore beneath his breath. It must be bad if Eric had put this woman ahead of their most important client. What the hell could he be thinking? Obviously, handing over the New York branch of the business to his half brother hadn't matured him any. "Do I know her?"

"Her name's Nikki Ashton. She's—"

"Head of Special Projects. Yes, I've heard of her. I don't think we've ever met, though." Jonah ran a hand across his nape, forcing himself to focus despite his exhaustion. "You hired her right after I left for London. What's she like?"

"She's a stunning woman, one of those leggy redheads."

"Loren," Della rebuked, "you know how much I hate it when you reduce people to the superficial."

He fingered his salt-and-pepper mustache and gave an apologetic shrug. "Sorry, darling. Old habits die hard."

"Get rid of her," Jonah recommended without hesitation.

Loren cleared his throat. "I'm afraid we can't."

"Why not?"

"The company needs her. For one thing, she's brilliant," Loren admitted. "And for another ... she's just been nominated for the Lawrence J. Bauman Award. The ceremony's in six weeks. How would it look if we fired someone of that caliber?"

Jonah's mouth tightened. Unfortunately, they were right. Businessmen and businesswomen nominated for the LJB Award were the most sought after in the country. It would cause irreparable harm to International Investment's reputation if they were to dump a potential winner on some trumped-up excuse. "Have you spoken to Eric about the situation?"

"No," Della admitted. "We kept hoping it would all blow over. You know Eric. He falls in and out of love more often than the wind changes."

"But not this time."

Della shook her head, tears gathering in her eyes. "She must be quite a special woman to hold his interest this long."

Jonah turned to face the windows. He knew Eric well enough to suspect which qualities needed to be so "special" to snag his half brother's attention for any prolonged length of time. If Nikki Ashton was a tenth as brilliant as Loren claimed, she'd have figured it out, as well...and she'd have used her wealth of riches to bring Eric to heel. He'd have been easy prey for a savvy—not to mention leggy—redhead.

"What about her husband?" Jonah questioned over his shoulder. "Or doesn't Mr. Ashton care that Mrs. Ashton is having a fling with her boss?"

"We don't know anything about him other than he's been out of the country for the past year," Loren confessed. "I don't even think his name is Ashton. She married about the time she started with us, but kept her maiden name. I checked with Personnel and Nikki never gave them any details. He's not part of her insurance or benefit program, either." He shrugged. "I'm afraid that avenue is something of a dead end."

"A modern marriage. How convenient," Jonah observed drily. He swiveled to face them, folding his arms across his chest. "Okay, Loren. What do you want me to do?"

"Couldn't you try to reason with Eric?" Della suggested before her husband had a chance to reply. "Or speak to Mrs. Ashton? If their relationship is causing as much trouble at the office as Loren fears, perhaps we could transfer one or the other."

"We have to be careful, Della," Loren replied with a frown. "I need Eric in New York right now. Aside from this incident with the Ashton woman, he's become a real asset to the firm."

"I've seen the reports," Jonah commented. "I'd hoped it meant he'd finally gotten his act together."

"Until this latest indiscretion he had." Loren shot his stepson a look of grim warning. "We also need to handle Nikki with kid gloves. She knows a lot about the company."

Jonah's eyes narrowed. "You mean she could do us some real damage?"

"If that's her angle," Loren confessed unhappily.

"Would you fly to New York and find out what's going on?" Della pleaded. Worry etched fine lines between her drawn brows. "Perhaps we're overreacting."

Jonah shook his head. "If anything, you're not worried enough. If Eric is serious about marrying this woman, she could be the worst thing that ever happened to him. But what if he's not serious? What if he loses interest in her? Would she want to even the score?"

Loren visibly paled. "I hadn't even considered that possibility."

"You'll fly out in the morning?" Della questioned, clutching Loren's arm.

"I'll leave now."

"But you must be exhausted," she protested. "You've just flown in from London. You need to sleep and—"

"I'm tough, Mother. Nor do I believe in jet lag." A tight smile touched Jonah's mouth. "Besides, I want to get to New York before Eric realizes I'm in the country."

New York City, New York

"What do you mean Eric's not here?" Jonah fought a losing battle with his temper. "Just where the *hell* is he?"

Eric's secretary squirmed in her chair. "I'm sorry, Mr. Alexander. He's...left."

"Left." Jonah planted his hands on her desk. "Could you be more specific, Ms. Sherborne? Where has he gone? And when will he return?"

"He had to catch a plane." She risked a swift, upward glance. "But I'm fairly certain he'll be back by Monday."

"Monday," Jonah repeated. Had someone heard he'd returned from London and warned Eric? "Was this a sudden trip?"

"Very sudden. I guess...I guess he had business out of town."

Judging by the nervous quiver in the woman's tone and the telltale flush invading her cheeks, the chances of Eric's disappearance having anything remotely to do with business were next to nil. "Where is he, Ms. Sherborne?" he demanded coldly.

"Um...I'm not certain of the specifics." She cleared her throat. "But he booked a flight to Las Vegas."

"*Nevada*? What business does he have there? We don't have any clients or investments in Nevada."

It was obvious that the secretary would rather be anywhere than pinned beneath his arctic stare. "Perhaps Mrs. Ashton's secretary knows," she finally suggested, the idea of passing him on to someone else clearly appealing to her. "Her name's Jan and her workstation is right across the hall."

Jonah stilled, fury gathering in his hazel eyes. "Mrs. Ashton's secretary is more familiar with Eric's movements than you are? Why is that?"

"Oh, no," she sputtered in alarm. "You don't understand. You see, Mrs. Ashton went to Nevada, too. Mr. Sanders didn't say where he'd be staying and I thought ... perhaps ... since the two of them were going together ..." She trailed off miserably.

Jonah stepped away from her desk, letting her off the hook. "You thought that since this was a *business* trip, Mrs. Ashton and Mr. Sanders might be sharing the same hotel, and that Jan would have the particulars. Is that right?" He made sure she caught the grim warning behind his explanation. One breath of gossip about this weekend tryst and her career at International Investment would come to an abrupt end.

Comprehension dawned in her wide eyes. Drawing a deep breath, she nodded. "Yes. That's exactly what I thought."

Without another word, he crossed the hall. Jan proved to be quite efficient. Although she didn't have any information about Eric's movements, she had all the pertinent details in regard to Nikki's. Within minutes, he had a copy of her itinerary and was booked on the next flight to Las Vegas. Which left one more vital chore, he decided grimly.

Ignoring Jan, he thrust open the door to Nikki's office and walked in, shutting it firmly behind him. The room was dim, the November sun fast becoming a chilly memory as the afternoon waned. It wouldn't be long before the Friday rush hour started in earnest. He didn't bother to check his watch to see how close he was cutting the drive to La Guardia Airport. He couldn't remember which time zone he'd set it for anyway. One thing he knew for certain—this little fishing expedition would have to be swift.

As he glanced around, a light floral scent assailed him, a perfume he'd never smelled before. It could only belong to one person. He inhaled deeply, feeling as though he drew Nikki's essence into his lungs. It wasn't the musky odor he'd have associated with a sultry redhead. Instead of black satin and lace, her perfume brought to mind a Victorian parlor filled with fresh flowers, sunshine and lemony beeswax.

He shook his head, amused. Clever woman. Something heavy and overtly sexual would have been too much of a cliché. Eric would have seen through that in a fast second. No, she was smart. Cloak a sexy package with an air of charming innocence and most men could be brought to their knees.

Crossing to her desk, he switched on a high-intensity lamp. It cast a blazing circle of white in the middle of the mahogany tabletop. Files were placed in neat, orderly stacks to one side, and just outside the pool of light stood a framed photo. Intrigued, he picked it up.

The picture of a young, laughing girl jolted him. He hadn't suspected that Nikki Ashton might have a child. Career women hot to marry the boss's son rarely came encumbered. He studied the photo. The girl couldn't be much more than five or six, her fine-boned features surrounded by a cloud of strawberry blond ringlets. She was held in the arms of a woman. Nikki? he wondered, curious. It was impossible to tell what the mother looked like. Most of her face was obscured by the child's flyaway curls. Only the woman's eyes and hair were clearly visible—china blue eyes brimming with laughter and her hair a shade or two darker than the little girl's.

It wasn't much to go on.

He returned the photo to its former position on the desk and glanced around, searching for any other personal touches that might reveal more about Nikki. But the desk—hell, the entire room—was practically barren, its decor austere and stark and unrelentingly tidy. His gaze came to rest on the one other jarring note to the office. A scraggly line of badly tended plants filled the window ledge. For some reason, the plants bothered him. A lot. They suggested some clue to her personality he couldn't quite pinpoint, but exhaustion and a relentlessly ticking clock kept the vital piece from taking shape. Later. He'd think about it later, when he had the time.

Besides, what could a bunch of half-wilted plants mean other than she had a black thumb and didn't care who knew it?

Finally, he turned his attention to the appointment book centered within the circle of light. He didn't hesitate to invade her privacy, but flipped rapidly through the pages. Tucked between Wednesday and Thursday he found a thick, gold-embossed envelope. It was empty except for a small rectangular card. He pulled it out, scanning it swiftly.

The Cinderella Ball, it read. *The Montagues wish you joy and success as you embark on your search for matrimonial happiness.* At the bottom was an address and the date of the ball.

It was today's date.

It didn't take long for the full impact to hit. Nikki had flown to Nevada to attend some sort of marriage ball. He thrust his hand through his hair. It could only mean one thing—Mrs. Ashton was now free of her unknown husband and available to marry. And Eric, without question, was her groom-to-be.

Jonah gritted his teeth. Well, not if he could help it. Because when he caught up with the beautiful, scheming Mrs. Ashton, she'd regret ever interfering with his family. He'd see to that.

Personally.

CHAPTER ONE

The Montagues' Cinderella Ball—Forever, Nevada

NIKKI ASHTON walked into the ballroom fighting to hide her apprehension behind a calm expression. There was no doubt about it. She'd clearly lost her mind.

How could she have believed that the solution to all her problems was marriage? And how could she possibly walk into this room full of strangers and find a man willing to play the part of her husband for the next few months? It was crazy. Insane.

And she'd never been so frightened in all her life.

She drew in a deep breath, then another and another. Ominous spots danced before her eyes.

"Hi," said a cheery-voiced woman.

Nikki turned blindly in that direction and discovered a waiflike pixie hovering at her elbow. "Hello," she said, amazed she'd managed to return the greeting.

"Care to sit with me for a minute?"

Afraid that if she didn't sit down, she'd fall down, Nikki sank into one of the clutches of seats lining the outer fringes of the ballroom. "Thanks," she murmured, dropping her purse onto the small table in front of her.

"I'm Wynne Sommers," the woman introduced herself.

"Nikki Ashton."

Bright green eyes peeked at her from beneath wisps of white blond hair. "Scared?" Wynne asked sympathetically.

For the first time in what seemed like ages, Nikki answered with the truth. "Terrified." She twisted her fingers together. "I'm not sure I can do this."

"But you have to, right? People are counting on you and this is the only option left."

Nikki stared at her companion in amazement. "How could you possibly know that?"

"I thought I recognized a familiar air of determination mixed with desperation." Wynne laughed. "It's the same for me."

"You *have* to marry?"

"I have two kids counting on me. If I don't marry, I lose them."

"I have relatives counting on me, too," Nikki found herself confessing. "Only I'm *trying* to lose them."

Wynne nodded sagely. "Some birds won't fly as long as Momma's there to feed them."

Nikki smiled in relief at the woman's instant understanding. "Something like that." She glanced around the crowded ballroom, pleased she could breathe again. "Have you been here long?"

"A couple of hours. The Montagues sure have a beautiful place. Have you met them yet?"

"When I first came in. They're a sweet couple."

"And their story is so romantic. Imagine being introduced to a complete stranger at a ball, falling madly in love and marrying that same night." Wynne sighed. "And here it is fifty years later and they're still every bit as much in love with each other as the day they met."

"I don't expect that to happen to me," Nikki insisted firmly. "I mean it's lovely of them to throw a Cinderella Ball every five years so others will have the same opportunity they did. And I'm sure there are plenty of people who find real love thanks to them. But it won't happen to me. I'm here for practical reasons. I have to get married.''

"So do I. Still..." Wynne cupped her chin in her hand. "I don't know why we can't have it all. I'm sure going to try. And did you know there's also an Anniversary Ball?''

"A what?''

"An Anniversary Ball. The Montagues throw a one-year Anniversary Ball for everyone who marries tonight.'' She sighed. "I'd sure like to go to that.''

"We have to get married first,'' Nikki reminded her. She gazed out at the glittering array of chattering men and women and fought the resurgence of her former panic. "I don't even know where to begin.''

Wynne offered an encouraging smile. "The first few conversations are the hardest,'' she said gently. "After that, it gets easier. Honest.''

"Have you had any luck finding someone?'' Nikki asked hesitantly, glancing at her newfound friend.

"Oh, I have my future husband all picked out. That's him over there.'' She inclined her head toward a tall, fierce-looking man chatting to a hard-eyed brunette. "Nice, huh?''

Nikki shivered. "Not really.''

"Don't let the tough exterior fool you,'' Wynne said with a quick laugh. "He wouldn't be much of a man if he didn't carry a bit of armor. He's a fighter, that one. Do you need a fighter?''

"He can't be a pushover, that's for sure,'' Nikki said, thinking of Eric.

"I'll tell you what. How about if you practice on my warrior? He won't mind. All I ask is that if it looks like he might be the one you want, give me the chance to talk him out of it. Okay?''

Nikki stared in astonishment. "Let me get this straight. You want to marry him, but you'll let me—"

"Have a go at him first. Sure." Wynne gave a careless shrug. "I don't think he's the man for you or I probably wouldn't offer. But he's a great icebreaker. He doesn't bother with a lot of social chitchat, just gets right to the point. Once he teaches you how to do it, the rest of the night will be a snap."

"I don't know...."

Wynne reached out and touched Nikki's arm. "Is marrying important to you?" she asked seriously. "Is it the most important decision you've ever made? Because if it isn't, go home."

"I can't," Nikki whispered. "I don't have any other choice."

"Then focus on that. It'll help get you through the evening. Look. The brunette is leaving. This is your chance. Go introduce yourself."

Nikki took a deep breath and stood. She couldn't say how or why, but in the past few moments, she'd regained control. She glanced down at Wynne. "Thanks," she said. "I owe you more than you'll ever know."

"Just remember our deal."

With a nod of agreement, Nikki headed toward Wynne's future husband.

Jonah glanced again at the card he'd confiscated from Nikki Ashton's desk, then at the cabdriver. "You sure this is the place?" he asked doubtfully.

"The Montagues' Cinderella Ball, right?" the cabby said in a bored voice. "That's where you wanted to go and that's where I've brung you. Just follow all those people. So's long as you stay on the walkway, you can't get lost."

Jonah gritted his teeth and tossed some bills onto the front seat before climbing out. Walkway or not, it would have been impossible to get lost. The damn place was the only building for miles around. It sat in the middle of the Nevada desert, outlined against the nighttime sky by colored floodlights and looking like some sort of giant platter stacked high with white-frosted cupcakes. He stared at the ridiculous architectural confection, then shrugged. What the hell did it matter? If it allowed him to get his hands on Nikki Ashton, he didn't care if it was built to resemble a bowl of whipped cream and cherries.

He worked his way through the crowd and into the mansion, pausing in the white marble foyer to get his bearings. A huge chandelier hung overhead, its soft light magnified by thousands of tiny prisms. Pine garlands embellished with twinkling fairy lights and white satin bows graced the massive Doric pillars that supported the thirty-foot ceiling. The flow of people continued around him and up twin, heart-shaped staircases. Taking a deep breath, he followed.

At the top of the steps he joined a reception line filing into the ballroom and only then realized that this ball required tickets for entry. He felt for his wallet, wondering if they took credit cards. Or perhaps he could bluff his way in. The throng moved steadily forward and within a few minutes he'd reached the head of the line. In front of him stood one of the most beautiful women he'd ever seen. She was tall and slender, her dark hair styled severely off her face. She held a basket of gold, waferlike tickets and offered a smile of greeting.

"I'm Jonah Alexander," he began. "Listen, I have a small problem—" But before he could utter another word of explanation, she suddenly focused on the next person in line. Her rich amber eyes widened in shock.

"Hello, Ella," a man's voice rumbled from behind.

Her face turned ashen. "Rafe," she whispered, and the basket of tickets tumbled to the floor.

Dropping to one knee, Jonah scooped handfuls of the heavy metal wafers back into the velvet-lined basket. With a muffled exclamation, Ella crouched beside him to help. "Are you all right?" he asked quietly.

"Fine," she insisted, though her trembling hands betrayed her. Gathering up the last ticket, she stood. "Thanks for your help."

"My pleasure."

He rose, too, and glanced pointedly at the man she'd called Rafe. He hadn't budged, but remained rooted in place as though he had all of eternity to wait. His cold gray eyes met Jonah's, leaving no doubt whatsoever that the situation with Ella was a highly personal matter. Still, Jonah wasn't one to back down from a fight. Using his height and breadth to secure his position in front of the woman, he turned his back on Rafe.

"Anything else I can do for you?" he offered deliberately, folding his arms across his chest. Unless she asked him to move, it would take a bulldozer to shift him from his stance.

Despair filled Ella's eyes. "I'm afraid not. Welcome to the Cinderella Ball. Enjoy your visit and we wish you a..." Her voice wavered, but she recovered swiftly. "We wish you a joyous future."

She'd as good as handed him his walking papers. And as much as he wanted to remain and help her out of whatever predicament Rafe represented, he didn't dare. He'd managed to gain entrance through sheer luck. He'd be a fool to push it. To his private disgust, he lingered anyway. Old habits, it would seem, died hard. "You're sure?" he asked softly.

Rafe stirred behind him. "Tell him to go, Ella. You know this is a private matter."

She gave Jonah a reassuring smile. "Rafe and I are old..." She hesitated, her smile turning bittersweet. "We're old associates. But thanks for your concern."

Jonah inclined his head. Sparing Rafe a final look of warning—and secretly amused at himself for bothering—he exited the reception line and plunged into the crowded ballroom. Despite the urgency of his own mission, if Ella had asked for his help, he'd have given it. He didn't have it in him to desert a woman in need. But since she hadn't asked...it was time to get down to business.

He had to find Eric and Nikki before it was too late.

Staring out across the packed ballroom, he realized what a monumental task he'd set himself. Finding his brother would be near to impossible—Eric wouldn't stand out among the multitudes, despite his slim height and gold-streaked hair. Jonah's eyes narrowed. But perhaps by zeroing in on the redheads, he could shake Nikki Ashton loose from the pack. And wherever he found Nikki, undoubtedly he'd find Eric, as well. Unwilling to waste another moment, he fixed on a possible candidate and began his pursuit.

Jonah leaned a shoulder against the wall and glared at the dancers twirling by. Damn it all! In the past ninety minutes, he'd waded through dozens of redheads in every shape, size and shade. And not one of them was Nikki Ashton. He stifled a yawn, struggling to throw off the exhaustion that dogged him. He needed more coffee—and he needed it bad. Check that. What he really needed was a few hours' sleep. If his mission wasn't so urgent, he'd call it a night and find somewhere to crash.

But it was urgent, and tired or not, he had to get on with it.

He took a deep breath, steeling himself to chase after the next redhead who floated by, when a tantalizingly familiar scent snagged his attention. It came from a woman several feet away. She had her back to him and was conducting an earnest conversation with a small, bookish individual. He hesitated, eyeing her upswept, Gibson girl hairstyle. She wasn't a bona fide redhead— at least she didn't have the brilliant sun-streaked red from the photograph. In fact, it didn't even come close. This woman's hair reflected the opulent darkness of polished mahogany, the color awash with vivid ruby highlights.

He started to dismiss her, but she shifted her stance, and her scent drifted by once again. If it wasn't the same perfume he'd smelled in Nikki Ashton's office, it was damned similar. Regardless, it roused his hunter's instincts and driven to act, he resumed the hunt.

"Ah, there you are," he interrupted her conversation with a lazy smile. "Sorry to take so long."

The woman turned abruptly, her gaze clashing with his. He'd made a mistake, he decided in that instant. This couldn't be the Ashton woman. Not only was her hair color all wrong, her eyes didn't match the china blue of the photo, either. Instead they were a velvety pansy blue, almost violet in their intensity. He'd accosted the wrong woman. Again. But this time he didn't give a damn. He was tired and angry and in desperate need of a ten-minute break—a break he intended to spend in the arms of a beautiful woman.

He slipped a hand around her waist. "You promised me the next waltz, remember?" he asked. Before she had a chance to argue, he inclined his head toward her companion. "Excuse us," he said without a trace of apology, and swung her onto the dance floor.

To his amusement, she didn't say a word, simply stepped into his arms as though she belonged. He was a tall man, but with her in high heels, the top of her head nestled just beneath his chin. Her scent wrapped around him and he closed his eyes, surrendering to the moment. She didn't pull away, but allowed him to mold her close, her lush curves settling into his as though they'd been specially made to fit. They danced in silence for several long minutes before curiosity drove him to look down at her.

Lord, she was a gorgeous woman. Her bone structure was exquisite, her creamy complexion bare of any freckles. She'd dressed all in ivory, the tailored jacket decorated with tiny seed pearls and crystal beads, and cut to accommodate her full breasts. She moved with ease, despite her short fitted skirt. But it was the glimpse of her long, shapely legs that caused a momentary qualm as he recalled Loren's description of Nikki Ashton. *She's a stunning woman, one of those leggy redheads.* Jonah frowned, eyeing his dancing companion speculatively. If he hadn't seen Nikki's picture, the woman he held in his arms could fit that description.

Then he caught sight of the wedding ring decorating her left hand and his gut clenched. Nikki was supposed to be married, too.

"This might be a good time to introduce ourselves," he suggested.

She shot him a wry look. "I assume that means we haven't met before, despite what you told Morey?" Her voice was as dark and rich as her hair, humor adding a musical note to her question.

"You caught me," he admitted, his mouth relaxing into a smile. "But it's an oversight I'm happy to correct."

"And I suppose that also means that I didn't promise you this or any other dance?" She glanced at him, amusement glinting in her eyes. "Did I?"

Those eyes intrigued him, the color an unusual blend of lavender and blue, the lighter portion of the iris ringed by a band of indigo. "Would you have forgotten if you had?"

She shook her head, a husky laugh escaping. "I suspect you'd be a hard man to forget."

It wasn't said flirtatiously, but with the cool candor of someone stating an indisputable fact. If he weren't so suspicious of her identity, he'd find her frankness appealing. "I'm Joe Alexander," he said, using the abbreviated name he'd assumed for the evening.

"Nikki Ashton," she replied.

It took every ounce of self-possession not to react, not to haul her off the floor and level her with accusations. The music ended just then, but his arms tightened around her. He hoped to hell Eric wasn't anywhere nearby or there'd be hell to pay. "One more dance."

Again she subjected him to that calm, assessing stare. "You aren't asking, are you?"

"No."

She hesitated, but before she could respond, the lights dimmed and the orchestra slipped into the next song. It was a slow, romantic one, chosen to encourage physical and conversational intimacy. Jonah gritted his teeth and molded her close, struggling to remain unaffected now that he knew who she was. She brushed against him as they drifted across the floor and his entire body clenched in response.

He wasn't the only one affected, he realized in the next instant. Delicate color tinted Nikki's cheeks and her breathing quickened. She wouldn't react to him like this if she were in love with another man came the furious thought. Unless, of course, she wasn't really in love. Curious to test his theory, Jonah slid his hand down the length of her spine, his palm settling into the hollow above her backside. The slightest amount of pressure set her tight against him.

And then he slowed their dance until it was no more than a pretext, a subtle form of foreplay. In the space of a few steps, it went from subtle to searing as her movements aligned themselves with his. He was practically making love to her right there on the floor—and she to him. Each step became part of a mating dance, her breasts crushed against his chest, her hips and thighs melded to his. She moaned, the sound barely more than a breathless sigh. But he heard it. He heard it and knew what she wanted.

"You feel it, too. Don't you?" he murmured.

"Yes."

The admission seemed torn from her. As though stunned by her own daring, she lifted her gaze to his, her eyes darkening like the sky before a gathering storm. But she didn't pull away, which only confirmed what he'd suspected. If she was in love with Eric, she wouldn't be responding to him. Not like this.

Determined to have final confirmation, he maneuvered her toward a dark corner. Their movements slowed until the gentle rocking motion was no more than an excuse to maintain as intimate a contact as possible. Her attraction was undeniable and impossible to ignore. Everything about her appealed—her full, lush mouth, her sunset-hued eyes, the rich auburn of her hair, the low, confidential pitch of her voice.

A small part of him fought to retain a clinical detachment. But as hard as he struggled to remember whom he held, that knowledge didn't change the intensity of his reaction. Whether he'd finally succumbed to jet lag or her allure outweighed his common sense, he couldn't tell. He only knew that he was driven by an instinct born in the male of his species millennia ago—an instinct urging him to abandon caution and take the object of his desire, by force if necessary.

Thrusting his hand into her hair, he tilted back her head and covered her mouth with his. He didn't ease into the kiss, didn't bother with preliminaries, but stamped his ownership in the most primitive way possible. She instantly yielded, offering sweet surrender in the face of his determined assault. It was that unexpected capitulation that almost sent him over the edge.

With an incoherent murmur, her lips softened, parted, encouraging him to plunder within. He didn't need a second invitation. He forged a union between them, mating his tongue with hers. She trembled in his arms, clinging to him as though he alone sustained her. And he, heaven help him, worshiped her with both hands and mouth. If they'd been anywhere but in such a public setting, he'd have taken what she offered with such unstinting passion. But he couldn't allow the burgeoning fire storm free rein.

Not here.

Not now.

Ultimately, it was that thought that restored his sanity.

With a muttered curse, he dragged his mouth from hers. He'd made a mistake touching her, he realized. Desire had given her beauty a wild edge and he couldn't help but wonder what she'd look like after a night of passion. Just the thought of her in his bed, her glorious hair spread across his pillows and her white, silken limbs entwined in his sheets almost destroyed his control.

Slowly, she opened her eyes and he saw then that she'd become a flame to his moth, a bewitching siren capable of enticing him to his doom. If his little brother saw them like this, he'd know what sort of woman he intended to marry. Whether she planned to line her pockets with Sanders money or she just hoped to advance her career, her reasons for marrying Eric had nothing to do with love. Jonah fought a surge of anger. The proof of that stood trapped within his arms, evidenced by the blatant desire reflected in a pair of pansy-soft eyes.

So where the *hell* was Eric? he wondered savagely. Why wasn't he here to witness the duplicity of his blushing bride-to-be?

His expression must have betrayed the violence of his thoughts. With a small murmur of dismay, she attempted to twist free. Jonah caught her close, not daring to release her. Not yet. Not until he decided what to do with her.

"Easy," he soothed, stroking her back. "Take it easy."

"Joe, please..."

There was a frantic note to the way she spoke his name and he knew what was coming. If he didn't act fast, she'd panic and run. And he'd never have the opportunity to uncover her plans for the evening. He slackened his hold, allowing her some breathing space while still keeping her within the circle of his arms.

"It's okay, Nikki. Just relax."

"Easier said than done." She drew a deep, shuddering breath. "Look, this was a mistake. Maybe—"

"Maybe we should make polite conversation for the next minute or two," he interrupted. "Would that help?"

She nodded in relief. "It might be wise."

"Fine. Let's see..." He fingered the cluster of pearls and crystal beads decorating her lapel. "You look stunning this evening. Very bridal." He used the word deliberately, hoping to guide the conversation toward Eric and their impending nuptials. To his surprise, her tension dissipated.

His increased.

Didn't it bother her that she'd just made passionate love to a complete stranger while her fiancé waited somewhere in the vicinity? A muscle jerked in his cheek. Apparently not.

She gave a self-conscious shrug, her gaze darting to meet his. "Isn't that the idea?"

"To look bridal tonight?" His eyes narrowed as he assessed the implications of her remark. Then he caught her left hand in his and lifted it until the overhead light sparked off her gold wedding band. "Most brides aren't already married."

"Sorry," she said with a wry laugh. "I've worn it for so long, I forgot it was there."

"I don't imagine your husband has forgotten."

"I don't have a husband. That's why I'm here."

"To get married," he clarified.

"Well, of course."

"And where is your groom-to-be?"

She'd recovered her poise and offered a cool, mysterious smile, so at odds with her fiery looks. "I haven't found him. Yet."

"And when he shows up?"

"Then we'll marry." A small frown touched her brow. "Isn't that how it works?"

His mouth quirked to one side. "Damned if I know."

"Look..." She moistened her lips, drawing his attention to their swollen fullness.

He'd done that, Jonah realized, or rather his kisses had. Here she stood waiting for her future husband while the taste of another man lingered on her lips. The anger that had smoldered just beneath the surface caught fire. What sort of woman was she? And why hadn't Eric seen through her? As though sensing that something about their conversation had gone awry, she stepped clear of his embrace.

"Perhaps this would be a good time to become better acquainted."

A harsh laugh escaped before he could prevent it. "I'd say the past few minutes pretty much covered that. Wouldn't you?"

His sarcasm didn't go unnoticed. She wrapped her arms around her waist in a defensive gesture. "I meant... Would you mind if I asked a few questions?"

"About what?"

"About you."

He eyed her with suspicion. "What do you want to know?"

She shrugged. "Why don't we start with the basics? Where are you from?"

"Originally? Chicago."

"And more recently?"

"Abroad."

That caught her attention. "You've been living overseas?" she asked with a delighted smile. "That's perfect. Will you be staying in this country for a while or—"

"My plans are indefinite." Impatience crept into his voice. "I should be able to wrap up the situation here in a week or two."

Disappointment drained the animation from her face. "I'm...I'm sorry to hear that. Is there any possibility you might alter your plans?"

What the hell was going on? Did she hope to arrange some future rendezvous? He glared in frustration, knowing he couldn't ask without tipping his hand. But damn it all, what about Eric?

"What is it you want?" he demanded bluntly.

She stiffened. "Nothing that will fit in with your plans, I'm afraid," she said, retreating behind a remote coolness.

"How the hell do you know that?"

She took a quick step backward, distancing herself still further. Jonah grimaced in annoyance, aware their rapport dissipated with each passing second. He'd screwed up but good and didn't have a clue how to make a graceful recovery.

"I'm based in New York," she explained. "If you were willing to move there, perhaps we could work something out. But—"

Work something out? Rage made him blind to everything else. He caught her arm and yanked her close. "Lady, I'm going to ask you one last time. What is it you're asking me?"

Alarm flared in her wide eyes. "I *was* asking if you'd relocate to New York. But now I just want you to let go of my arm."

Slowly, he released her and stepped back. It had to be exhaustion. There couldn't be any other excuse for his behavior. "Sorry," he muttered, thrusting a hand through his hair. "I didn't mean to hurt you."

"Forget it," she retorted. "Now if you'll excuse me, I need to find my future husband." And with that she turned on her heel and walked away.

CHAPTER TWO

NIKKI swept across the ballroom, determined to put as much distance between her and Joe Alexander as possible. Never in her entire life had she lost control like that. She fought to draw a deep, steadying breath. What could she have been thinking? Control was everything to her.

And she'd lost it the instant he'd put his hand on her.

Lost it? Hah! She'd given it up without so much as a token struggle.

She shook her head. How could she have been so foolish? Since the day her parents had died, she'd been forced to take charge of her odd assortment of relatives—Krista and Keli, Uncle Ernie and Aunt Selma, her cousins.... They all routinely turned to her with their problems. And with cool, calm logic, she'd resolved every single one they'd dumped in her lap. Even when her work situation had turned problematic, she'd found a solution without asking anyone for help.

She was proud of that. Proud of the fact that no matter how desperate the circumstances, she'd never become emotional, never failed to choose a course of action and never, ever lost her cool.

Until tonight.

She risked a quick glance over her shoulder. Joe stood where she'd left him—apart from the glittering crowd, his arms folded across his chest—watching her with a fierce green-tinged gaze. She looked away, shaken. What had just happened? One minute she'd been kissed to within an inch of her life, and the next he'd treated her as though she were beneath contempt. It didn't make any sense.

She balled her hands into fists.

More than anything, she wanted to forget him and move on to the next man. But she couldn't. Joe was too fascinating. From the moment he'd intruded on her conversation with Morey, she'd been utterly spellbound, walking into his arms as though she'd been born to do so.

Was it his eyes? she wondered. They were such an odd shade of hazel—flashing green fire one moment, before darkening to a crisp golden brown the next. Or perhaps it was the keen intelligence she'd glimpsed in his stare, the instinctive knowledge that he'd fought his way through every single one of the years marking his hard, chiseled face. Whatever it had been, it had ignited an answering spark in her. Even when a cold sharpness had settled in his gaze, he'd still managed to hold her captive.

"Excuse me," an earnest young man interrupted, tapping her shoulder. "Would you care to dance?"

Unable to concoct a plausible excuse for refusing, she reluctantly slipped into his arms. She'd have time for regrets later. But not now, not when she had business to attend to. It was growing late and she still hadn't found a suitable husband. Unfortunately, Joe Alexander had succeeded in destroying what little enthusiasm she'd managed to summon for the job. She suspected it would be a challenge to find anyone else who came close to matching him.

She glanced at her current partner and struggled to muster some interest. He was a handsome man. Very handsome. In fact, his features bordered on the classic. Best of all, his rounded jaw didn't so much as hint at an annoyingly stubborn nature. Nor did he have thick, winged brows that notched upward in silent demand for answers to unreasonable questions. He also lacked that penetrating stare that stole every thought from her head.

Instead, his nose was arrow straight—no intriguing little bump to suggest a barroom brawl. His lips were on the narrow side—no wide, sensuous mouth capable of stealing soul-altering kisses from unwary women. And he had a soft tenor voice—no deep, rumbling bass tones that echoed through her mind long after the words had died.

He was quite, quite perfect.

And quite, quite boring.

She sighed. This had to stop! She had to quit comparing every man she met to Joe. She risked another brief look at her current dance partner, determined to find something that appealed. His hair was a pleasant enough shade of brown, but a degree or two darker than Joe's and lacking the startling sun-bleached streaks. Nor did this man's height compare. At a guess, Joe stood several inches over six feet. Broad shouldered and built along rock-solid proportions, he eclipsed most of the men she'd spoken to so far that evening, including this one. She'd never met anyone who exuded quite such an air of power and authority.

So what in the world had gone wrong?

"My name's Dan Forsythe," her dance partner announced at length.

She broke off her analysis long enough to reply, "Nikki Ashton." Was it something she'd said that had annoyed him?

"It's a pleasure to meet you."

Something she'd done?

"Er...the song's ending."

Something she didn't say or do?

"Would you...would you care to talk for a few minutes? Nikki?" He stopped dead in the middle of the floor. "Ms. Ashton?"

She blinked. "The song ended."

He looked at her oddly. "Yes. And I thought we could take the opportunity to talk. You know. Get better acquainted."

Nikki released a quiet sigh as they left the floor. How different from Joe's more aggressive approach. But then, if Dan had swept her off to a darkened corner and attempted to kiss her, she'd probably have slapped his face. "What is it you're looking for in a wife?" she asked, deciding to be blunt.

"Children," he blurted with awkward enthusiasm. His gaze slipped from her face to a spot somewhere behind her and then back again. "Do you like kids?"

"I'm afraid I'm not ready to have a baby," she confessed gently. "At least not yet."

"Oh."

His focus continued to shift to a point somewhere behind her with nervous regularity. She refrained from turning around, but couldn't help wondering if he'd found someone more appealing. She cleared her throat to regain his attention. "The problem is, I have a career."

"Then kids are out, huh?"

She hesitated. *Forget Joe!* she told herself sternly. *Concentrate on the business at hand.* She'd known all along that certain concessions might be necessary to achieve her goal. Her problem with Dan mirrored many she faced at work—two parties with similar ambitions but with differing needs and objectives. She just had to find an equitable solution to their dilemma. "I wouldn't say children are out, precisely."

"Still, you're not interested in having any." He looked behind her again while at the same time edging backward. "Are you?"

If she didn't do something fast, she'd lose him. "Perhaps we could reach a compromise," she offered quickly. "If you were willing to wait a while to have children—"

"Forget it. I...I guess we're just not compatible. It was nice meeting you." And with that he vanished into the surrounding crowd.

She frowned. That was odd. Why had he kept looking behind her? He'd almost acted as if... Her eyes narrowed suspiciously. He'd almost acted as if he were intimidated by something. Or some*one*. She spun around, not in the least surprised to discover Joe standing nearby. He held a glass of champagne, which he raised in salute when their gazes clashed. Why, that dirty, rotten... Hadn't he done enough harm allowing her to believe he was interested in her when he wasn't? Why did he have to chase off those who might be sincere?

Snatching the arm of the closest available male, she offered a dazzling smile. "Care to dance?"

To her relief, he didn't flat out refuse. But the next ten minutes proved to be the most arduous of her life. It didn't take any time at all to discover he was a pompous ass looking for a wife whose qualifications roughly equaled those of a maid. Worse, he danced in a tight little circle so that every few seconds she came face to face with Joe.

The instant the dance ended, she excused herself, determined to find a better scouting location—one that offered a suitable array of potential partners and yet *didn't* contain Joe Alexander. Unfortunately, she lost out on both counts. Over the next thirty minutes, her situation progressed from bad to worse. It didn't matter whom she spoke to or where she went—there was Joe. Several times he blatantly listened in on her conversation, making her so nervous she couldn't even string a coherent sentence together.

Finally, she couldn't take any more. Determined to put an end to his harassment, she excused herself from her latest disaster and crossed to confront him. She wouldn't give up control as she had before, she told herself. This time she'd take command of their conversation. And no matter what, she wouldn't allow him to touch her.

He greeted her with a lazy smile, a smile directly at odds with the hard glitter in his eyes. "Having fun?"

"No, I'm not. And it's all your fault. Why won't you leave me alone?" she demanded. "What do you want?"

"From you? Not a thing."

"Then why are you following me?"

"Curiosity."

"*Curiosity*?" She blinked in surprise. "But why? You had your chance to work something out between us. You blew it. So why can't you go away and let me find a husband?"

He stilled, eyeing her intently. "Is that what you're doing? Looking for one?"

"I'm trying! But you're making it rather difficult. You keep scaring them off."

She could see him analyzing her answers, considering them as though they were puzzle pieces that didn't quite fit. His brows notched upward and she knew what that meant—another of his impossible questions. "Tell me this..." He fixed her with an irritable glare. "Are you meeting your future husband here or not?"

"Yes, of course," she said. "Or I will be if you stop interfering."

"When and where will you meet him?"

"How would I know that?" she retorted, exasperated. "I'm not a fortune-teller."

He frowned. "I'm a bit confused. I was under the impression that you were waiting for someone specific."

She planted her hands on her hips. "I am. I have very specific qualifications, and for your information, you don't meet a single one." Honesty forced her to concede, "Well, maybe one or two. But not the important ones."

The predatory gleam returned to his eyes. "Perhaps we should discuss the ones I do meet."

"Forget it," she muttered.

Jonah came to a decision. He still didn't know whether or not she was waiting for Eric. Unfortunately, as much as he preferred the direct approach, he couldn't simply ask, not without revealing a suspicious amount of ignorance. But he needed answers. And one way or another, she was going to provide them. "Arguing like this isn't helping either of our situations. We need to talk. Truce?"

She hesitated. "I don't know.... It's getting late and I can't afford to miss this opportunity. If we can't work something out, I've lost a lot of time."

"I won't keep you long." His hand settled on her shoulder. "Why don't we go outside and talk?"

He didn't give her a chance to think of an excuse, but opened a pair of French doors leading to the gardens and ushered her through. It was cool outside, though not uncomfortably so. Slate stepping-stones marked pathways that twisted in and out of exotic trees and shrubs, their presence an incongruous touch in the Nevada desert. Splashes of moonlight revealed tables and benches half-hidden in the leafy vegetation. Few were occupied, but Jonah wanted to insure their privacy and led her deeper into the garden.

In the far recesses, they approached a table tucked snugly beneath a tree covered in twinkling fairy lights. The couple who'd been sitting there were just leaving. The man tucked a set of papers into his suit coat pocket and planted a possessive arm around the woman. She peeked out from beneath white blond hair and exchanged a smile of recognition with Nikki.

"Good luck," she whispered before being whisked along the pathway toward the mansion.

"A friend of yours?" Jonah asked curiously.

"We met earlier in the evening," Nikki confessed. "I was a bit nervous and she sat and talked to me for a while."

"Why were you nervous?"

She shrugged. "This is a pretty big step, don't you think? I suppose I was having second thoughts about the wisdom of going through with this sort of marriage."

This sort of marriage? What the hell did that mean? He waited until she sat down before joining her on the bench. Enough was enough. The time had come for answers and he intended to get them, no matter what it took. "This is a rather unusual party," he probed carefully.

"Until I read the article, I'd never heard of anything like it," she agreed. "Imagine throwing a ball for people who want to get married."

So he hadn't misunderstood the card he'd found on her desk. This *was* a marriage ball. Still, he suspected he hadn't quite gotten the full picture. For instance— where was Eric? "That's how you found out about it?" he prompted. "From an article?"

"Yes. It was in our local newspaper." Her smile glimmered in the darkness. "My sister showed it to me. She found it highly amusing."

"But you didn't."

Her smile faded. "No," she admitted. "It struck me as the perfect solution." ·

"Solution to what?"

An innocent enough question, yet it clearly hit a nerve. She clenched her hands, the fairy lights in the trees above ricocheting off her wedding band. "It's... it's a long story," she said at last.

"I have all the time in the world." He didn't exaggerate. He was determined to find out what the hell was going on, even if it took all night. "Talking about it might help."

She hesitated, and he could tell she was debating whether or not to answer. "I suppose complete honesty might be best... all things considered."

"I gather you don't always feel that way."

She turned her head sharply at the disapproval coloring his words. "Normally, I believe in honesty above all else," she asserted, her tone growing notably cooler.

"But whatever your story is—it involves a lie," he retorted. He didn't attempt to placate her. He couldn't. Not when she'd lied about something—something that might affect Eric's well-being.

She didn't hesitate. "Yes," she admitted. "It does."

"Tell me about it."

He endured another brief silence while she gathered her thoughts. Even in the short amount of time they'd spent together, he had noticed that quality about her— her control and precision, the care she took before speaking. She'd be a tough one to break, should it come to that.

"It's my own fault," she began in a low voice. "I never should have lied about being married."

Of all the possible confessions he'd expected to hear, this one didn't come close to making the list. "What did you say?"

She held out her hand, and her wedding band winked in the subdued lighting. "You asked me about this earlier. What I didn't explain is...it's pure decoration. I'm not married." A whisper of a laugh escaped. "I'd hardly be here if it were real, now would I?"

He was at a loss to answer that. Not until he found out more about this ball. "Then why the pretense?"

"The company I work for prefers married executives."

Who the hell had told her that? "So you decided to accommodate them?"

"I played with the idea. But not too seriously. At least not until—"

"Until?"

"There's a man at work. He's very sweet. Young."

"He's interested in a personal relationship with you?" Was that possible? Could Loren and Della have misunderstood the situation? Or was Nikki Ashton just a damned good liar?

"He's more than interested."

"I still don't understand. You faked a marriage because you couldn't tell him no? Isn't that a little extreme?"

"Not when the man in question is my boss."

He stood. The way she said it—with such detached candor—convinced him she spoke the truth. At least the truth as she saw it. *Damn Eric!* What the hell had he instigated? "Why are you here?" he demanded.

She tilted her head to look up at him and the silvery moonlight caressed the pale beauty of her face. Her expression appeared calm and serene. But her eyes gathered in the shadows surrounding them, their fathomless depths hinting at untold secrets. "I'm here for the same reason you are. To meet someone compatible enough to marry."

"Couldn't you do that in New York?"

"Possibly. But courtships are often lengthy affairs. By attending the Cinderella Ball, I can meet someone, we can marry tonight and return home in the morning. Problem solved."

He must have misunderstood. After almost thirty hours without sleep, it was a distinct possibility. His mouth tightened. He'd better have misunderstood, because he didn't like the sound of this at all. "The people attending this party...that's why they're here? To marry complete strangers? They meet, choose someone at random and marry—all in *one night*?"

"Of course," she responded, surprised.

"Of course." He realized then that she was serious. Dead serious. "If that's true, you people are in desperate need of reality checks."

She frowned, her brows arching in question. "Now *I* don't understand. Aren't you here because you want to marry?"

He had no intention of answering that one. "Let's focus on you right now," he suggested. "We can discuss my situation later." He didn't give her time to respond, but continued with his interrogation. "You're marrying because your boss won't take no for an answer. Is that about the size of it?"

"There's a personal reason, as well."

"Which is?"

Her lashes flickered downward, concealing her expression. "As I said...it's personal."

He fought to hide his impatience. "So because of this personal reason and because you can't handle your boss any other way, you're going to marry a complete stranger."

She inclined her head, the rich auburn tones muted by the darkness. "I know. It sounds insane. But you see, everyone already thinks I *am* married."

He folded his arms across his chest, a hint of sarcasm creeping into his tone. "And since they do, you're going to turn this fiction into fact. That makes sense."

"I have no choice," she retorted, stung. "I'm not interested in acquiring a husband. Ever." She drew back into the shadows, her voice low and pained. "At least not for something as illusionary as love."

That gave him pause. "If that's how you feel, then why go through with such a crazy scheme?"

"Because it's the perfect solution."

"That's open to debate."

Her temper flared again. "This isn't some half-cocked plan I've devised," she told him. "I've given this marriage idea a lot of thought. Aside from needing to resolve a private dilemma, I have a boss who thinks he's in love with me."

Jonah looked at her sharply. "And is he?"

"No. Eventually, he'll realize that for himself. But until he does, I need the protection of a real husband."

"How is this husband going to protect you from..." Damn, he'd almost slipped up. "What's his name?"

"Eric." She released her breath in a long sigh. "It won't be easy. I need someone sophisticated. Someone mature. Someone intimidating. Part of the problem is that I've told everyone that my husband has been out of the country for the past year. Unfortunately, it's left the impression that our marriage is in trouble."

"So you need a man who can dispel those doubts," Jonah said slowly. "With a real husband on the scene—someone who can act the part of a passionate spouse—Eric will realize there's no future in a relationship and get over his infatuation."

"Exactly."

"So where's the problem? If you're actually committed to going through with this crazy idea, why haven't you married already?"

Her laugh was half groan. "The problem is that no one I've met so far meets my qualifications. Either they're sweet, lovely gentlemen whom Eric would rip to shreds in no time or they're strong, independent types with their own agendas. And those agendas don't include moving to New York for the duration of our marriage."

"I can't believe that there isn't someone—"

"No? What about you?" She leaned forward, her gaze never wavering from his. "I can offer a home, a car and a modest salary. It doesn't even have to be a permanent arrangement. There was a man I met this evening who wanted a temporary wife. If you prefer, I'd be willing to agree to a short-term marriage, as well. I'll hire you to be my husband for whatever period of time is convenient, under whatever terms you deem fair, so long as my predicament with Eric is resolved by the time we get an annulment."

"Isn't this a little extreme? Can't you—" He broke off as a sudden thought struck him. "This Eric . . . is he harassing you? Has he said something—done anything—inappropriate?"

"No, no, nothing like that," she answered immediately. "He's . . . kind. Protective."

Jonah gave a short laugh. "Yes, I can see where that might be a problem."

"It's not funny! He's never touched me, at least not in any suggestive way. But I know how he feels." The iridescent seed pearls decorating the bodice of her suit jacket sparked with each agitated breath she drew. "I'm not imagining all this. I'm not!"

He held up his hands. "All right. I believe you. But tell me, how do you know it's personal? Isn't it possible you've mistaken friendly concern for something more serious?"

She shook her head. "I wish that were the case, but it isn't."

"Convince me."

Her gaze flashed to his. "I don't know why I should have to."

"You're the one desperate for a husband. Convince me you really need one."

Again she took her time considering his request. After several tense moments, she inclined her head. "Very well. Can you tell when a woman is attracted to you?"

"Sometimes," he admitted. "If she's obvious about it."

"Well, Eric has been very obvious. Right from the start he signaled his interest."

"What did you do?"

"I...I told him I didn't share his feelings and that mixing business with pleasure was always a mistake. Needless to say, he thought he could convince me otherwise, and that's when I made my first mistake."

"You lied."

"Yes. I said I was engaged. Afterward, he remained...hopeful." She shrugged. "I guess he thought he could change my mind. So out of desperation, I showed up one Monday morning wearing a wedding ring.''

''Your second mistake,'' Jonah informed her caustically. ''Didn't the wedding ring slow him down?'' Unless his brother had switched personalities this past year, it should have.

''Yes, it did. He seemed to accept the futility of a relationship.''

''But something happened to alter that. What?''

''A company banquet. I came alone, claiming that my husband was out of the country. Eric went along with it for the next several weeks. He'd even tease me about my husband's prolonged absence. But as time passed and I never brought him to any company functions, Eric changed.'' She hesitated as though searching for the appropriate description. ''He became indignant on my behalf, and later angry. I think the anger changed to suspicion when I didn't share his distress. He senses I'm hiding something, and I suspect he's hoping my marriage is on the rocks.''

''That still doesn't mean—''

''There's more,'' she interrupted. ''He confides in me, although I do nothing to encourage it.''

Jonah tensed. ''What does he talk about?''

''His family. Mostly his older brother—how much he admires and tries to emulate Jonah, how it feels to lurk in someone's shadow, how tough it is to live up to a legend.''

''Sounds like he sees you more in the light of a mother confessor than a potential lover.''

''I wish that was all it were. But if I get too close to him, I can see how he fights for control. And when he looks at me...'' She shook her head. ''I can't explain it, except to say that a woman is able to sense these things.''

Jonah had heard enough. "So you see marriage as the only solution."

"I don't like it, but I have no choice. I have to find a way to correct the situation before it gets any further out of hand. It's starting to affect our work. We're both making mistakes and eventually someone is going to catch on. I can't afford to lose this job. It's too important to me." She stood and approached. "Joe, please help me. Will you...will you marry me?"

He knew how much it cost her to ask. But that didn't change his answer. "No."

"Why not?" Desperation crept into her voice. "What is it you want?"

"What I want isn't at issue right now. Look, Nikki, you have two choices. You can go through with this ridiculous scheme to marry or you can do the smart thing."

"And what's the smart thing?"

"Tell Eric the truth. Tell him you faked a marriage because you didn't want any romantic complications at the office. Tell him you're not interested in anything other than work and that you want him to leave you alone. Ask for a transfer."

She spun away, wrapping her arms about her waist. "I can't."

"Why not?"

"Do you really think it's so easy?" Her temper flared, stirring the passions she obviously kept under such tight control. "I'm supposed to waltz into work and make this big announcement, and then what?"

"Then you're off the hook."

"No, I'm not. By the end of the day, it's all over the office that I lied about being married because I couldn't handle the situation with my boss any other way. By the end of the next day, our clients have heard about it, and by the day after that, so have our competitors. It would do incalculable harm to my reputation, Eric's reputation, as well as damaging the credibility of our firm. We'd be a bad joke. Thanks, but no thanks. Anything is preferable to that, even marriage."

Her attitude toward marriage bothered him. A lot. Perhaps if he'd had time to sleep on it, he might have been in a position to offer a more palatable solution. But since he didn't have that luxury... "Come on." Slipping a hand beneath her elbow, he drew her close. "Let's go."

"Where?"

"To find you a man. If you're so determined to buy a husband, I'll help you shop for one."

She resisted the pull on her arm. "I don't understand. Why are you doing this?"

"Let's just say I'm a sucker for a hard luck story."

"But what about you?" she protested. "It's getting late. Aren't you worried you'll miss your chance to find a wife?"

"Believe me, finding a wife is the least of my worries." The very least. He stopped in the middle of the walkway. "What's the problem, Nikki? Having second thoughts?"

A momentary hesitation disturbed the even tenor of her expression. It was quickly masked by a steely resolve. "No. I'm not having second thoughts."

"Then let's go."

The next hour only served to prove Nikki's point. No one they approached quite suited her needs. Most Jonah dismissed as being too weak. She was right—Eric wouldn't see them as a serious obstacle to his pursuit. If anything, he'd think he was doing her a favor. And those who would have held him at bay had their own requirements—which meant a wife to fulfill their criteria, not the other way around.

"There's a guy over there I haven't spoken to yet," Jonah said without much enthusiasm. The man in question was too old, too fat and too desperate. Eric would make mincemeat of him. But time was growing short.

"Don't bother," she replied with a shiver. "How about—" She broke off, her face paling. "Oh, no!"

"What is it? What's wrong?"

She twisted around, practically throwing herself into his arms. "Quick! Hold me."

His arms closed around her automatically and he tucked her close. His hand skated down the length of her spine, molding her more firmly against him. She felt like heaven, soft and warm, her unique scent filling his lungs. If he hadn't believed in jet lag before, he sure as hell did now. There couldn't be any other explanation for his reaction. It was too intense, too surreal.

Her breath came in quick, panicked bursts and he lowered his head close to her ear. "What is it, Nikki? What's wrong?"

She lifted her face, her mouth inches from his. For a crazy instant he thought she intended to kiss him. Then he saw her expression. Stark disbelief registered in the pansy blue of her eyes. "Eric's here," she whispered.

CHAPTER THREE

"I CAN'T believe it," Nikki exclaimed. "How did he find me?"

Jonah grimaced. He had a fairly good idea. The all too efficient Jan seemed a safe bet. He chanced a quick look toward the reception area. Eric stood there, an earnest expression on his face, talking to the Montagues. Undoubtedly, he was attempting to charm his way into the ball. And knowing Eric, he had every chance of succeeding. Jonah swore beneath his breath. The situation was more serious than he'd suspected.

A lot more serious.

"Come on." He dropped an arm around Nikki's shoulders and swept her through the nearest doorway.

She'd turned ashen, her eyes huge and desperate. "What am I going to do now?"

Jonah set his jaw, trying to decide. He'd been a fool to drink even a single glass of champagne—particularly when he hadn't slept for a day and a half. Right now he'd kill for a hot shower and eight solid hours between the sheets. Maybe then he could figure out an appropriate course of action. But tonight his exhaustion made that near impossible. Not that there were many avenues available to them. In fact, he'd only come up with one.

"It would seem we're out of options," he informed her. "If he's this determined, you need to marry someone he can't intimidate."

"We've canvassed just about everyone here." She scanned the assembly with an air of urgency. "Who's left?"

"Me."

It took a full minute for that to sink in. Astonished, she turned to look at him. "But you said—"

"Forget what I said."

"You're willing to marry me?" she asked in disbelief. "Why? I mean, don't think I'm ungrateful, but..." Skepticism gradually replaced her surprise. "Why would you be willing to help me now when you wouldn't before?"

"I ignored one damsel in distress this evening," he said with a hint of self-mockery. "It just isn't in me to ignore another."

"I won't claim to understand what you mean by that."

"That's a relief." He offered a bland smile and indicated a corridor leading to a back staircase. "Shall we get this over with? We'll need a marriage license. I overheard someone say they're being processed downstairs in the library."

A small frown puckered her brow and she shook her head, indicating she wouldn't be so easily persuaded. He almost laughed aloud at the irony. Here he risked alienating his entire family to resolve a problem *she'd* created—and she still wasn't satisfied. If she'd just told Eric no from the start, instead of concocting this whole ridiculous scenario, they wouldn't be in their present predicament. Now, if he wanted to ensure his brother's well-being, salvage the jobs of two of International Investment's key personnel, as well as straighten out their hopelessly muddled personal lives, he'd have to take serious action.

"I know I'm not in a position to argue," she was saying.

"That's for damned sure."

She rebuked him with a look. "I do, however, have a few concerns."

He released his breath in a gusty sigh. "Naturally."

"First…I expect you to convince Eric we're a happily married couple. Can you do that?"

His eyes narrowed as he absorbed the slight. The mere fact that she needed to ask underscored her lack of faith in his abilities. Not many could have offered such an insult and escaped without repercussions. "I'll convince him that if he approaches my wife with anything other than business in mind, he'll regret it." He allowed a hint of his displeasure to show. "Or don't you think he'll believe I'm serious?"

She held his gaze for a tempestuous five seconds before looking away, color sweeping into her cheeks. "He'll believe you," she concurred.

"Fine. Let's go."

She dug in her heels. "Wait a minute. I'm not through."

He ground his teeth. "Lady, I said I'd marry you. What more do you want?"

"I just need to make sure we understand each other."

He grimaced. "Trust me, I understand more than you realize."

"I'm talking about specifics. I don't want any dispute later on."

"Then you'd better talk fast because I'm giving you precisely thirty seconds," he informed her tightly. "After that, you're on your own."

Apparently, she took his warning seriously. Without wasting any further time, she ticked her questions off on her fingers. "Okay. You've already agreed to convince Eric we're a happily married couple. Second...you're willing to move to New York, right? You'll stay with me until the situation with Eric is resolved?"

"Yes."

"Third...you understand that your actions mustn't put my job in jeopardy?"

"I understand." He folded his arms across his chest. "Is that it? Are you through now? No fourth, fifth or sixth on your list?"

"Just a fourth."

"Which is?"

If he hadn't caught the turbulent glitter in her eyes, he'd have thought her completely unaffected by their discussion. After all, she'd rattled off her points like some sort of human computer. But that flash of deepening violet gave her away. Whatever her final point concerned, it should have been first on her list, not last.

"I need to know your expectations."

He lifted an eyebrow, surprised by her request. He'd anticipated something far more crucial. "I expect to marry you, save your bacon and then send you on your merry way," he replied. At the same time, he'd protect International Investment from any further business debacles and allow Eric time to come to his senses.

"And that's all?" She moistened her lips. "You won't ask any more of me?"

Comprehension dawned, and with it came a purely masculine reaction, a predator's response to spotting its prey unprotected and vulnerable. He stepped closer, his attention drawn to the pulse fluttering frantically at the base of her throat. "Are you asking if I want to sleep with you?" he questioned deliberately.

She retained her cool, although he suspected it was a hard-fought battle. "Yes. I guess that's what I'm asking."

"I don't think it's worth discussing."

To his amusement, she looked relieved. Did she misinterpret all business discussions as badly as this one? he couldn't help but wonder. He'd have to speak to her about that. He couldn't afford to have the company put at risk because of her erroneous assumptions. "Now, have we addressed all of your concerns?"

"Yes."

"Then I suggest we get this over with before your boss succeeds in talking his way past the Montagues and tracks us down." He shot her a sharp glance. "He doesn't know the purpose of this ball, does he?"

"I don't think so. I told him I was flying out to meet my husband," she explained, then eyed him uneasily. "I don't know why he followed me. Maybe he was curious to meet you..." She released her breath in an exasperated sigh. "My husband, I mean."

"Or maybe he didn't believe you were really meeting anyone. Let's just hope the Montagues don't go into lengthy explanations about their reason for throwing this little shindig or we'll be up to our necks in it." He took her arm in an iron grip. "Let's find the library."

Footmen dressed in white and gold uniforms directed them downstairs to a county clerk who processed the marriage licenses. She wore a name tag that read, "Dora Scott." Discarded on one side of her desk was a sign announcing, "For faster service, feed me hors d'oeuvres." A short line had formed in front of her, but by the time they'd filled out the necessary applications, the room had emptied.

"Let's see who we have here," Dora said as they approached. She held out her hand for their forms.

Realizing he stood on the brink of disaster, Jonah hastened to introduce himself. "It's Joe. Joe Alexander." Nikki might not associate the abbreviated form of his name with Eric's half brother. But his given name was unusual enough that if Dora blurted it out, his identity would be all too evident. And he had no intention of revealing his connection to Eric until after they were safely married.

The clerk glanced at his application and chuckled. "Fine, *Joe.*" She examined the second form. "And Nicole."

"Nikki," the bride-to-be hastily corrected. She indicated the sign. "I'm afraid we didn't bring any hors d'oeuvres."

"Forget it. One more cheese puff and I'd probably pop. Okay, folks, let's get through this." Within minutes, Dora had typed up the necessary paperwork and handed them a thick blue-and-white envelope. "Marriage ceremonies are conducted in salons off the main ballroom. Give the envelope to whoever officiates. You get to keep the fancy-looking certificate inside as a souvenir. But it's not a legal document. That comes later in the mail." She glanced at them. "Any questions?"

"Not a one," Jonah responded.

Dora nodded. "In that case, I have one piece of advice. Take care of each other, hear?"

"Taking care of people is what I'm best at," Nikki assured the clerk.

"Funny," Jonah muttered. "That's what I was going to say."

"Swell. A pair of caring souls," Dora said with a laugh. "Get out of here, the both of you. You need to get hitched and I have work to do."

"We better make this quick," Jonah advised as they returned to the ballroom. "If Eric managed to talk his way in, I don't want to run into him at an inopportune moment."

Nikki paused outside the door to the first salon. "It seems we have a choice of ceremonies. What sort do you prefer?"

"The short-and-to-the-point sort."

He shoved open the nearest door and looked inside. Nikki caught a glimpse over his shoulder and made a small sound of disappointment. Not that he blamed her. The room was attractive, but very stiff and formal. Even when the judge beckoned him to come forward, he hesitated. For some reason, he found ice blue brocade, walnut furniture and artificial flowers a total turnoff. Besides, it wouldn't suit Nikki.

He backed out and closed the door. "Bad choice," he announced.

"What's wrong with it?"

"Too long a line," he lied, fully aware that from her angle she hadn't seen enough to dispute his verdict. "Let's try another."

Opening the door to the next salon, he nodded in satisfaction. It was perfect. Tiny and intimate, it had an old-fashioned, almost Victorian feel to it. A dainty Laura Ashley rose print covered the walls, and the overstuffed couch and wing chairs were finished in a deep ruby velvet with ivory lace arm covers. Centered along one wall was a cherry highboy displaying an ornate silver tea service. Along the other was a fireplace with a gold-leaf beveled mirror above the mantel that captured an overview of the entire room. Fresh flowers filled delicate Waterford crystal vases, the fragrance of roses offset by the smoky scent of hickory from a gently crackling fire.

If he could have chosen the perfect setting for Nikki, it would have been one like this.

She stepped into the room behind him and caught her breath in delight. "Oh, Joe, this is wonderful."

"It'll do," he agreed with a lazy smile, not quite certain why the setting for a temporary marriage mattered so much. He must be more exhausted than he'd thought.

A minister rose from a chair beside the fire and smiled at them, his thick white hair reflecting the leaping flames. "Welcome. I assume you wish to be married?"

"Yes, please," Nikki answered without hesitation. "Right away, if you don't mind."

The minister smiled indulgently. "Very well, my dear. But before I begin, I'm required to ask that you give careful consideration to what you're about to do."

Jonah nearly groaned. If he did that, he might come to his senses and back out. No, better they get this over with and fast. "Look, we've considered, we've decided and we're in a hurry." He thrust the envelope containing the necessary forms at the minister. "Could you just get on with it?"

The minister accepted the envelope and adjusted the wire-rimmed glasses perched on the end of his nose. "I'm afraid not," he replied, his gentle blue eyes turning somber. "You see, marriage is a serious commitment, not to be entered into lightly. So I ask that you face each other and look carefully at your partner. Make sure that your choice is the right one."

Cursing beneath his breath—but realizing it was the only way they'd get this show on the road—Jonah turned to look at Nikki, studying her with clinical detachment.

At first, all he noticed was her appearance. Tall and beautifully proportioned, she was a stunning woman. Her translucent violet-flecked eyes met his without flinching. He liked that about her; he had from the start. Of course, there were other qualities he liked, as well.

Her mouth was the most kissable he'd ever encountered and her skin the softest he'd felt in an age. Even the deep auburn of her hair suited her to perfection. He half smiled in appreciation as he eyed her elegant topknot. Sometime during the evening, glossy tendrils had escaped to curl with fiery abandon about her temples and the nape of her neck.

And that's when he saw beneath the surface.

Her hairstyle mirrored her nature, he suddenly realized. She struggled to attain the appearance of severity and restraint, but couldn't quite achieve it. Equally, she fought an unending battle between the tempestuous aspects of her nature and the need for rigid control. On the surface, she appeared perfectly composed. But underneath smoldered an inferno that probably terrified her, that threatened the calm, orderly existence she'd built. With new insight, he looked at her again. And in the end it was those pansy-soft eyes that gave her away—betraying her uncertainty, her desperation, her passion, as well as her unwavering strength and determination.

He wanted this woman.

He wanted to feed those sparks of inner rebellion, to release the delicious fire she kept tamped inside and to be scorched by the heat of it. Keeping all those emotions bottled up couldn't be good for her, and he decided then and there to find a way to demolish her control. Hell, he'd probably be doing her a favor.

In the meantime, he had to find a way to alleviate her
fears. As though in response to his thought, the scent
of roses drifted to him again. He turned and crossed to
the nearest vase, stripping a few sprigs of baby's breath
from the arrangement.

"Come here," he ordered gruffly.

She crossed to his side, hesitating a few feet in front
of him. He closed the distance between them and very
gently arranged the baby's breath around the loose knot
crowning her head. Her hands slipped across his chest
to cling to the lapels of his black suit coat as she waited
for him to finish. She wouldn't be happy when she discovered his identity, he realized with regret. But he hoped
to convince her that what he'd done was in everyone's
best interest.

At least, that's what he told himself.

Nikki stared up at Joe, scrutinizing the taut, uncompromising planes of his face. She hardly dared to breathe
as he tucked the flowers in her hair. Satisfied, he looked
at her, a reassuring tenderness glittering in his eyes. And
with that one look, all her fears dissolved.

She'd been so nervous, the enormity of her decision
almost overwhelming her. When the minister had suggested they reconsider the step they were about to take,
she'd almost fled the room. Not even her desperation
over Eric could have dissuaded her from backing out,
even at this late hour. Only the memory of Krista—and
that overheard phone conversation—held her rooted in
place.

But looking into Joe's hazel-green eyes and seeing his
confidence and self-possession went a long way toward
easing her uncertainties. He must have known how close
to the edge she'd come, for he leaned down, his breath
mingling with hers.

"Don't worry," he whispered in reassurance. "I'll take care of everything."

Cupping her face, he sealed his vow, his mouth capturing hers in a gentle kiss. She opened to him, the last of her misgivings fading within the protective strength of his arms. It would all work out. With Joe at her side, she could solve all her problems.

Reluctantly, he released her. "Any more doubts?" he asked.

"None."

"Then will you marry me, Ms. Ashton?"

A tremulous smile teased the corners of her mouth. "Yes, Mr. Alexander. I will."

"Have you reached a decision?" the minister asked.

"Please begin the ceremony," Nikki requested, perfectly calm and collected. Perfectly willing. "And it's Joe and Nikki."

With a rakish grin, Jonah plucked a single rose from the nearest vase and handed it to her. At her questioning look, he shrugged. "A bride should have a bouquet."

The ceremony was surprisingly brief, as per their request. Just before the minister pronounced them husband and wife, he peered at them over his spectacles. "Would you care to exchange rings?" he asked. "We have them on hand. They're tokens, really. Just something to use until you're able to replace them with the genuine article."

"I already have a ring," Nikki told Jonah in a hesitant undertone. "Everyone would think it strange if I wore something different now."

"Give it to me."

She slipped it off her finger and dropped it into his outstretched palm. "What about you?"

"I'll need a wedding band."

The minister dutifully fetched a tray of rings. The third one Jonah tried fitted. To her surprise the design on his ring almost matched her own. In fact, if she didn't know better, she'd have believed it to be every bit as real. Even more real was the moment he slipped the ring onto her finger. It was a moment out of time, a brief instant in which their marriage attained a veracity and permanence she hadn't expected.

It isn't a permanent marriage, she tried to tell herself. *It's only temporary.* But the image of their exchanging wedding bands became fixed in her mind, an indelible snapshot that she knew she'd carry for a long time to come.

And as the minister pronounced them husband and wife, Nikki realized she was in deep, deep trouble.

It wasn't until they'd reached her rental car that Nikki's earlier doubts crept back. Had she done the right thing? Had she married the right man? *Had she lost her mind?*

"So where do we go from here?" Jonah asked once they were confined in the dark interior of the sedan.

"I have a room at the Grand Hotel. It's not too far from here." She fought to keep her voice even and nonchalant. "I . . . I thought we could spend the night there before returning to New York in the morning."

"My ticket's open-ended," he said with a shrug. "Flying out tomorrow is fine with me."

"Are you staying at the Grand, too?"

He shook his head "I wasn't sure what to expect tonight so I booked a room in Las Vegas."

He didn't know what to expect? That didn't make sense. Surely he expected to find someone compatible and marry her. "Why—"

"How about—"

She smiled at the momentary confusion, her tension easing. "Sorry. Go ahead."

"Since your hotel is closer, why don't we stay there?"

Filing her question away for the moment, she gave her attention to the matter at hand. "What about your luggage? Would you like to pick it up now?"

"I don't see the point. We can take care of it on the way to the airport tomorrow. In the meantime, I'm sure your hotel can provide me with the bare essentials. To be honest, what I could use more than anything else is a bed."

She hoped he didn't mean that the way it sounded. Reaching for the ignition, she cast him a quick, suspicious glance, but it was too dark to read his expression. "You must be tired," she commented pointedly.

He caught her hand before she could start the engine. "Don't let your imagination run away with you." Amusement rumbled in the deep tones of his voice. "As much as a wedding night with you appeals, sleep appeals even more."

"I knew what you meant," she snapped, annoyed that he preferred sleep over her—and even more annoyed that she'd find anything objectionable about that fact.

She started the car, the engine roaring as she gave it far too much gas. Damn it! Why had everything turned so awkward? If only she could pretend he was a difficult client. She'd always been assigned the tough ones. It was her métier and one of the primary reasons she'd been put in charge of special projects at International Investment. In every instance, she'd used her analytical skills to figure out what the client wanted, then cool, calm reason with a touch of charm to negotiate from there.

She gnawed on her lip. Unfortunately, Joe was her husband, not a client. And she suspected that neither charm nor reason would cut much ice with him if he decided to be difficult.

She pulled onto the road leading to the hotel, determined to remain in control of the situation. After all, she wasn't interested in him as a man, at least not sexually. Her reaction to those kisses could be explained away as purely hormonal. That was it. It could be chalked up to a normal, healthy reaction any overworked, stressed and desperate woman would have to a virile, violently masculine, wildly sexy male animal. It had nothing whatsoever to do with a growing emotional attachment. She'd learned her lesson the hard way in that particular arena.

Emotional attachment led to pain and disillusionment and financial ruin.

Logic and control kept her world safe and protected.

All she needed was a husband to help resolve her problems with Eric and Krista. Once they were settled, she and Joe could get an annulment. Then she'd be free—free to simplify her life and pursue her career. In fact, she'd be able to give her full attention to work and not worry about anything else. That would make her happy. Right?

"You okay?"

"I'm fine," she insisted with a too-bright smile. "I'm looking forward to starting a new life. Off with the old and on with the new and all that."

"Yeah, right."

She turned into the hotel parking lot and suddenly remembered his earlier comment. "I've been meaning to ask... why didn't you know what to expect?"

He shook his head as though to clear it. "What?"

"A few minutes ago. You said you'd booked a room in Vegas because you didn't know what to expect at the Cinderella Ball."

"Did I?" He gave a weary shrug. "I must be more tired than I thought. I don't remember saying that."

She pulled into a parking space and turned off the ignition. "You did. To be exact you said—"

"I guess I wasn't certain I'd find anyone who would suit," he cut in decisively. "I didn't know what sort of women to expect at the ball."

It wasn't until they were in the elevator that she found the flaw in his response. "I still don't understand," she began.

"What don't you understand now?" He spoke calmly, yet she caught a betraying flash of autumn gold in his cool gaze.

"You didn't have any conditions."

He leaned against the back wall and folded his arms across his chest. "Come again?"

"Conditions." She frowned as the elevator panel blinked its way through the lower numbers. "I asked what you wanted out of the marriage and you didn't have a list. Every other man I spoke to had some requirement or request or need." She turned to look at him. "Except you."

"So?"

The door slid open and he gestured for her to proceed. "So...you're intelligent. And you're good-looking in an uncompromising sort of way," she itemized slowly. "That much would be obvious to most women who met you for the first time."

"Gee, thanks."

Recalling the passionate kiss he'd laid on her, she conceded, "Unfortunately, you're a bit on the aggressive side.'' Though he certainly knew his way around a woman's mouth. She glanced at him from beneath her lashes, deciding to keep that particular asset to herself.

"I'm a man, not a marshmallow. Aggression comes with the territory."

"You're also argumentative," she shot back. "But without a list, you're easy to please. That's your best quality, in case you didn't know. So why didn't you think you'd find someone to suit?"

"I guess I have a pessimistic nature."

"So do I, but I was still fairly confident I'd find *someone*."

He stopped in the middle of the hallway and held out his hand. She stared at it blankly. "The key," he prompted in dangerously soft tones. "For the door."

"Oh. It's a card, not a key."

His hand didn't budge. "The card, then."

Reluctantly, she dug through her handbag and gave him the thin strip of plastic. "What I'm trying to say is…you never showed any interest in other women after you danced with me. In fact, you spent the whole time helping me find a husband instead of looking for a bride."

"What room?"

"Eighteen-twenty. You spent all that money to attend the Cinderella Ball and you didn't find a wife."

Reaching the appropriate door, he slid the card into the slot. The light on the steel plate by the knob flickered from red to green and the lock snicked open. "I believe that wedding ceremony we just went through means I found a wife." He thrust open the door. "After you."

She hesitated. "But I'm not a real wife. And you never explained. Exactly why did you need to get married?"

A muscle jerked in his jaw. "You're a real enough wife as far as I'm concerned. And I didn't." He planted his hand in the small of her back and ushered her firmly across the threshold. "Need to get married, that is."

"You didn't?"

She spun around as the door swung closed. He stood in front of it, a large, impregnable barrier. For the first time, she realized that aggressive men could also be intimidating—especially when the man in question was her husband. Perhaps if they were in an office instead of a hotel room and it was a business meeting instead of her wedding night, she wouldn't have felt so nervous. But he had such a grim expression on his face. She clasped her hands together, aware that her confidence was rapidly ebbing.

She cleared her throat. "If you didn't need to marry, then why...?"

"I didn't *need* a wife," he repeated, stepping away from the door and stalking into the sitting area toward her. "Not everyone gets married because it's the only way out of a tight spot. Some people actually marry for more pedestrian reasons. Like companionship. Or children. Or even love."

She fell back several steps, her eyes widening. "Is that why you wanted to get married? For love?"

"Why the sudden interest, Nikki?" His question had an edge she didn't like, a raspy quality that spoke of exhaustion and frustration and anger. "We had all night to talk. You could have asked these questions at any point during the evening. But you didn't give a damn about anything except solving your own little predicament. So why bring it up now?"

The sitting area that had seemed so spacious when she'd first entered the room had grown dramatically smaller. "I...I just wondered why you married me."

"Because solving your problem solves mine."

"I don't understand."

He stripped off his jacket and tossed it over a nearby chair. "I don't expect you to. Yet."

Before she could question him further, he took a final step in her direction. Retreating an equal distance, the back of her knees hit the edge of the bed and she sat down abruptly.

"It's a king-size bed," she explained in a rush, scooting backward on the quilted cover. "When I realized the mistake, I tried to get two doubles, but the hotel's full. Every room's taken. I thought maybe the couch..." She gestured wildly toward the sitting area.

"You're not using the couch and neither am I." The mattress dipped beneath his weight. "We're husband and wife now, remember?"

He trapped her beneath him before she had a chance to roll away and she stared at him in shock. "But you claimed we wouldn't... You didn't intend..." Frantically, she searched her memory, struggling to recall his exact phrasing. "You said you didn't want to sleep with me!"

"I told you it wasn't worth discussing. And it's not. Certain issues are non-negotiable, and this is one of them." His eyes were a fierce green, glowing with blatant desire. "So no more discussion. No more negotiations. The time has come for action."

"No—"

"Yes, Mrs. Alexander. Most definitely, yes."

Framing her head with his hands, he stole a gentle kiss, confirming her earlier opinion. Dear heaven, but he knew his way around a woman's mouth. He also knew when to coerce and when to coax. And right now, he coaxed. Teased. Tempted.

Seduced.

Hot little flames flickered to life again, splashing across her skin, seeping deep within to weaken every muscle and sear every nerve ending. She tried to resist, to explain all her reasons for keeping their relationship platonic. But the words were lost, swallowed by a far greater need—a need that consumed all rational thought.

The buttons of her suit jacket fell open and his mouth drifted downward, following the length of her throat. She teetered on the edge of surrender. He was her husband. He was helping her resolve an untenable situation. And she wanted him. Heaven help her, she wanted him. Considering the circumstances, could making love be so wrong?

"Nikki," he muttered in a passion-slurred voice. "I'm sorry. I can't resist."

"I know," she whispered. "I feel the same way."

"Thanks for understanding."

His shadowed jaw rasped across sensitive skin and she held her breath, aware that she'd committed herself to folly. He cupped her breasts, nuzzling the curves above her lacy bra and then...

Nothing.

"Joe?" she murmured, shifting beneath his oppressive weight. He didn't respond, and as the seconds ticked by, desire waned. She moistened her lips, the return of sanity making her extremely self-conscious. "Are you sure about this?" she asked uneasily. "Don't you think we should wait until we know each other a little better? Joe? *Joe?*"

And it was then she realized he'd fallen fast asleep.

CHAPTER FOUR

NIKKI stirred, two disparate sounds bringing her to full consciousness.

One was the familiar hiss of a shower.

The other was a tentative knocking at the door.

Neither made any sense to her. But then, until she'd had two strong cups of coffee, not much did first thing in the morning. She rolled onto her back and blinked up at the ceiling, struggling to recall why the bedroom looked and felt so strange.

And then she remembered—remembered everything.

She darted a quick, nervous glance toward the far side of the mattress. Joe wasn't there, only a depression in the bedding confirming he'd spent the entire night beside her. That explained the sound of running water. Her— she swallowed hard—*husband* must be in the shower. Another knock sounded at the door the same instant as the flow of water stopped.

Confronting the unknown entity in the hallway seemed a safer bet than confronting the well-known entity toweling off after his shower, she decided. Kicking back the covers, she pulled on her robe and went to answer the summons. With luck, Joe had ordered breakfast before closeting himself in the bathroom. Thrusting an unruly tumble of hair from her face, she unlocked the door and tugged it open.

"Hi, Nikki." Eric stood there, an abashed grin on his face. "Surprise."

She whipped the door partially closed and ducked behind it, glaring at him through the remaining two-inch crack. "What are you doing here?" she demanded in a furious whisper. "Have you lost your mind?"

"Is that room service?" Joe's deep voice rumbled from close behind. "I'd kill for a cup of coffee."

"It's not room service," she replied without turning around. Speaking softly, she ordered, "Go away!"

Eric's jaw dropped. "I'm not going anywhere until you tell me what the hell my brother is doing here."

Her eyes widened in alarm. "Who? Where?"

"Right there behind you! My brother, Jonah. What's he doing in a hotel room with you? And dressed like that, no less!"

She spun around and literally went weak at the knees. Never in her life had she seen such an appealing sight. Joe stood in the middle of the room wearing nothing but a fluffy white towel. His skin was golden, his chest an endless expanse of dark brown fur, and he stalked toward her with the determination of a gladiator ready to join battle. Everything about him exuded power. From the resolute expression in his autumn-hued eyes to his wall-like shoulders to his solidly muscled legs, he approached with the grace and assurance of a seasoned warrior. And all she could do was stand and wait, uncertain of the rules of engagement in this particular war.

Reaching her side, he wrapped his arms around her. "Morning, sweetheart," he muttered in his distinctively raspy voice and nuzzled the side of her neck.

She gasped at the torturous pleasure his stubbled jaw kindled. "Joe, what is—"

"Don't say a word," he cut in tersely. He spoke close to her ear, his quiet warning conveyed with a harshness that stunned her. "Just play along or I swear you'll regret it."

She opened her mouth to protest, but as though anticipating that, he kissed her. It was long and slow and deep, stealing every thought from her head. Unable to help herself, she relaxed, her body turning pliant and eager within his embrace. How did he do it? the rational part of her mind wondered. With one kiss, he demolished every hint of resistance and turned her from a reasonable, logical, intelligent woman into a helpless puppet. How was it possible?

"*What the hell is going on here*?" Eric shouted.

Nikki started, having completely forgotten about his presence. But Joe—or was it Jonah?—didn't even twitch. Taking his time, he finished the kiss before lifting his head. He grinned down at her, flicking his finger across her rosy cheekbone.

Finally, he addressed Eric. "Hello, little brother. Here I manage to sneak off for a romantic weekend with my wife and you still find a way to track me down. How'd you do it?"

Eric fought to draw breath. "What— When—"

Jonah released a gusty sigh. "It was Jan, wasn't it? She spilled the beans." Shooting Nikki a reproving look, he ruffled her already-ruffled hair. "You've got to get better control over that secretary of yours, sweetheart. What could be so urgent that we can't have a private weekend without business intruding?"

"I—" Her mouth opened and closed like a stranded fish.

Without missing a beat, Jonah returned his attention to Eric. "And just what is it that's so urgent?"

"I didn't— I thought—"

"I'll tell you what," Jonah interrupted. "There's a restaurant downstairs. Order up a large pot of coffee while we dress and we'll join you for breakfast as soon as we can." He didn't wait for Eric's reply, but slammed the door shut in his brother's face.

"What the *hell*—"

Jonah cupped his palm over her mouth. "Wait!" he snapped in a curt undertone and cocked his head meaningfully toward the door. Hustling her to the sitting area at the far end of the room, he removed his hand. "Okay, finish."

"Is going on?" she concluded in a furious whisper. "Just who the hell are you?"

"Your husband."

"That's not what I mean and you know it! You're not Joe Alexander, are you?"

"No."

He folded his arms across his chest, drawing her attention once again to the corded muscles of his well-developed arms and the impressive width of his shoulders. Lord, he was gorgeous, she reluctantly conceded. And distracting as the devil. She closed her eyes to block out the sight, focusing once again on the business at hand. "You're Jonah Alexander? Eric's brother?"

"Yes. I shortened my name so you wouldn't recognize it."

She'd figured out that much already, but it still came as a distinct shock to hear the casually stated confession. She sank into a chair, staring at him in disbelief. "*Why?*"

A cynical light turned his eyes a chilly golden brown. "Can't you guess?"

With his standing there in nothing but a loosely knotted towel? Not a chance. "Maybe if you dressed," she suggested faintly.

His mouth curved in amusement. "I will—just as soon as the clothes I ordered from the men's shop downstairs are delivered. No luggage, remember?"

She bowed her head to avoid looking at him. "I still don't understand," she said through gritted teeth.

"What in particular is giving you trouble?"

She could hear the laughter in his voice and resented it passionately. "What's going on? Why were you at the Cinderella Ball last night? Why did you marry me?" A sudden thought occurred and her head jerked up, her hair spilling across her shoulders in a riotous tangle of sable brown and deep russet. "We are really married, aren't we?"

"Oh, we're legal all right."

"But you used a fake name—"

"I just used a nickname, same as you. If you'd bothered to look at our marriage license, you'd have seen Jonah Alexander spelled out in all its glory." His tone was dry, his gaze mocking. "From there it would have been a simple enough leap to connect me to Eric."

"If I had, I'd never have married you," she retorted bitterly.

"No doubt."

"And you still haven't answered my questions."

He ran a hand across his shadowed jaw and she remembered how his day-old beard had abraded her skin when he'd nuzzled her neck. Mild pain had melded with a more profound pleasure. The result had been electrifying and she eyed his jawline speculatively. What would it be like to feel that tantalizing scrape against her breast? An intense warmth unfurled in the pit of her stomach at the mere thought and she clenched her hands, fighting the unwanted sensation.

"Well?" she snapped.

He shrugged. "I came to the Montagues' to stop you from marrying Eric."

"*What*? I wasn't planning to—"

"I know that now."

"But you didn't last night," she stated with dawning comprehension.

"Not until after we'd conducted a rather lengthy conversation."

"The one outside in the garden." His strange behavior the previous evening began to make sense. Finally. "That's why you were asking all those odd questions and kept pestering me about my prospective bridegroom. You didn't understand the purpose of the ball."

"Not entirely," he conceded.

"What in the world did you think I was doing there?"

"Meeting Eric."

"I can't believe this," she muttered, dragging a hand through her hair.

"The evidence was damning," he explained without apology, "especially the part about you and Eric flying to Nevada on International Investment business—"

"We don't have any business interests here," she inserted automatically.

"I'm well aware of that fact." He waited a beat before adding, "And so is the rest of the office staff."

She couldn't hide her dismay. Apparently Eric's pursuit of her had left ample room for conjecture, not to mention gossip. "But we weren't traveling together," she argued. "I didn't even know Eric had followed me until he showed up at the Montagues'."

"The bottom line is that you both flew to Nevada. You both had reservations here at the Grand. And there'd already been talk of an affair. In this case, two and two may have added up to five, but to an outsider it sure as hell looked like an elopement."

"You were leaping to conclusions," she said dismissively.

"Was I? Don't forget one other detail—the Montagues' Cinderella Ball. The few facts I'd ascertained suggested it was some sort of gala for couples who wanted to marry. And when I called the Grand, they confirmed that most of their guests were attending and gave me directions. I'd have booked a room here, but they were full by then."

Her eyes narrowed suspiciously. "How did you find out about the Cinderella Ball?"

"You left the announcement on your desk."

"You searched my desk?" she demanded, outraged.

"If you're expecting an apology, you've got a long wait," he said with callous disregard. "I had a job to do and I did it."

"So you came out to Nevada believing Eric and I were going to marry and bent on stopping us, right? Why? What difference did it make if I married your brother?"

"Aside from the fact that I believed you were already married and that you have a few years on him?"

She lifted her chin. "Yes. Aside from those reasons."

"Your... relationship had begun to affect your work. You acknowledged as much last night. Why do you think Loren called me home?"

Her eyes widened in alarm. "The Sanderses—your parents—know?"

"What they know, or rather thought they knew, was that Eric was having an affair with an older, married woman. The affair had become common gossip among the employees and had distracted the principals involved to the point that they almost succeeded in losing the Dearfield account.''

"Oh, no!''

"Oh, yes,'' he responded with brutal deliberation. "I recommended they fire you. If you hadn't been a nominee for the Lawrence J. Bauman Award, you would have been.''

"Why?'' she demanded. "Because I had the temerity to catch the eye of the boss's son?''

"No. Because you allowed your personal life to interfere with business.''

"So it was Jonah Alexander, troubleshooter, financier extraordinaire and former LJB winner to the rescue. Is that it?'' She didn't bother to hide her resentment.

"That's it.''

"And your solution was to marry me?''

"Not by a long shot. You were the one who settled on that as a solution. I merely accommodated you.''

"Why?''

For the first time, anger disturbed the even tenor of his voice. "What choice did I have? I couldn't change your mind about marrying and you wouldn't settle on an acceptable husband. Then Eric showed up and it was either marry or expose you as a liar.'' He stepped closer, his expression falling into grim lines. "But believe this, *Mrs. Alexander*, if I didn't think that revealing the truth might damage the reputation of International Investment, I'd have given you up in a heartbeat and damn the consequences.''

"I had to do something about Eric,'' she protested.

"You didn't have to lie. If you make such foolish decisions in your personal life, I have to wonder what the hell you're doing on the job."

The criticism struck hard and cut deep. "My work is beyond reproach!"

"Except for the Dearfield account, you mean?" came the harsh retort. "Well, we'll find out, won't we?"

"What are you saying?" she asked apprehensively.

"I'm saying that I intend to analyze your performance over the past year. And if I find anything out of sync, LJB Award or no, you'll be out on that pretty little tail of yours."

She leaped to her feet, her hands balling into fists. "If that's how you feel, why did you bother to marry me?"

"You think I wanted to?" His anger erupted with tangible force, reflected in the taut line of his jaw and the hot sparks of gold flaming to life in his eyes. "Our marriage is an inconvenient means of salvaging an untenable situation. And you, my accidental wife, are a temporary encumbrance."

"How dare—"

"Oh, cut the self-righteous indignation," he snapped. "You used me last night every bit as much as I used you. What did you say? It wasn't just Eric but some personal matter you needed to resolve, as well?"

His reminder stopped her cold. How could she have forgotten Krista and Keli? "Yes," she conceded, her anger fading as swiftly as it had flared.

"Well, at least Eric won't be a problem any longer."

She stared in confusion. "Why not?"

"He won't poach," Jonah stated succinctly. "After this morning, there won't be any doubt in my brother's mind that not only are we married, but we share a passionate relationship. If I read him right, he'll be furious at you for not telling him the truth about us. Any feelings he might harbor should die a swift and bitter death.''

She turned her back on him, blinking hard. She'd never wanted to hurt Eric, only ease an uncomfortable situation. But everything she'd done so far only succeeded in exacerbating matters. "How do we explain our marriage to him?" she asked quietly.

"We say that we became engaged before I left for London and we married a short time afterward on one of my trips to the States. We kept it quiet because we didn't want it to affect your position at work." His voice acquired a cynical edge. "We'll tell him you preferred to make it on your own. He should buy that.''

Her mouth tightened. "Go on.''

"We're celebrating our one-year anniversary by renewing our vows at the Montagues' party and had planned to make the big announcement to the family immediately afterward.''

"You have it all worked out," she said, unable to conceal her resentment.

"Somebody had to.''

"I'll have you know I had complete control of the situation." She turned to face him. "Your interference wasn't necessary.''

"You had it all under control?" She couldn't mistake his sarcasm. "Which part?''

"Once I married—''

"Fine. Let's start there. Never in my life have I heard of anything as crazy as this Cinderella Ball. You really intended to marry a complete stranger?''

"Yes." She strove for nonchalance. "What's wrong with that?''

"What—" He bit off a curse. "You knew nothing about me. Not even my real name. I could have been an ax murderer. Or worse."

"What's worse than an ax murderer?" she muttered.

"Don't tempt me to show you. How could you be so irresponsible?"

"I'm sure there were no ax murderers present," she argued. "The Montagues ran security checks. They had all the guests investigated before they authorized their invitations."

"A fat lot of good that did."

His voice had become dangerously soft, the bass tones rumbling with stormy threat. His hand closed around her arm and he tugged her close. She made a small sound of complaint, not that he noticed or cared. Instead, he secured her against him, the thin cotton of her nightgown providing as flimsy a barrier as his towel. She splayed her hands across his chest, her fingers sinking into the generous pelt of hair to the taut layer of skin and muscle beneath.

"Joe—Jonah, please. You don't understand. It was perfectly safe."

"Really? Well, for your information, *wife*, I didn't have an invitation. I walked right in the front door and no one made a move to stop me. Now tell me again how everyone was investigated and deemed safe. Am I safe? Well? *Am I*?"

She stared into blazing hazel eyes, the strength of his fury impacting with stunning force. More than anything, she wanted to look away. But she didn't, compelled to meet that impossible gaze while still retaining the tattered scraps of her control. "No," she replied tartly, remembering his attempted seduction once they'd returned to the hotel. "You aren't the least safe. Last night proved that beyond any doubt."

"Did it?" His eyes narrowed as he considered her comment and she regretted ever having made the dig. "After thirty-odd hours without sleep, some of it's a bit hazy. I don't recall much toward the end, except—"

"Nothing happened!" she broke in defensively.

A hint of jade green crept into his curious gaze, and a slow smile creased his mouth. His arms slid around her, his hands settling on her hips. "That's not quite the way I remember it," he said, easing her close.

Struggling was out of the question. She hardly dared so much as breathe for fear of the consequences. "I thought you couldn't remember anything."

A quiet laugh broke free. "I don't. At least not much. My last memory was falling asleep on the softest, fluffiest pillow I've ever set cheek to." Color flamed in her face, and his gaze drifted from there downward, settling on the agitated rise and fall of her breasts. "I wouldn't mind trying it again."

"Let go of me." If anything, his hold tightened and she was terrified that he might kiss her. If that happened, she'd be lost, just like every other time he'd touched her.

And he knew it as surely as she.

"I don't recall much after that." His brow wrinkled. "I sure don't remember undressing. And yet when I woke up this morning, someone had taken off my shoes." He cocked a gold-tipped eyebrow. "You?"

"I may have."

"And my shirt?"

A sudden image of the night before came to her. Once she'd gotten over her initial shock and anger at his falling asleep, she'd been unable to just leave him sprawled on the bed, fully dressed. He'd looked too uncomfortable. The shoes had been easy. The shirt less so because he'd worn a cummerbund. Never having seen a man put on such a device, let alone attempted to remove one, she'd wrestled with it for endless moments before locating the hooks. Added to which, he'd been so huge, it had taken every ounce of strength to roll him over enough to take care of the problem.

"You haven't answered my question," he prompted.

"Once I figured out how your cummerbund worked, the shirt was a snap. I put your cuff links on the dresser, by the way."

She didn't add how unnervingly intimate the procedure had been. Finding the buttons within the folds of his dress shirt hadn't seemed so bad; his body heat singeing her through the soft cotton, though, had come as a distinct shock. He'd lain stretched across the bed, his shirt gaping, hers to touch and care for. She'd hurried initially, desperate to get the job done. But as she'd worked the shirt off his shoulders and arms, her movements had slowed. And heaven help her, she'd been unable to resist caressing that incredible musculature. Did he know? Did he suspect that she'd traced every hard curve—the deep furring of his chest, the taut ripples of his abdomen, the beautifully sculpted biceps?

She risked a quick upward glance, but his expression told her nothing. He held her so close the crisp hairs of his chest brushed the curve of her jaw, swamping her with desires she'd never known she possessed—desires she didn't dare communicate to him. They were the same feelings that had spilled through her as she'd unbuttoned his trousers. She'd panicked then, just as she was almost panicking now. Last night, she'd bolted from the bed and locked herself in the bathroom for a long, hot shower. Afterward, she'd thrown a blanket over his slumbering form and crawled into bed next to him. Curling into a tight ball as far to one side of the king bed as she could manage, it had taken her a long, long time to drift off to sleep.

"Where have you gone, Nikki?" he questioned softly.

Her gaze flew to his and she shook her head, unable to answer. For where she'd been, she didn't dare allow him to follow. To her eternal relief, a knock sounded at the door, sparing her the need to invent a response.

"I think this conversation might be worth pursuing further," he said.

"I disagree." She stirred within his hold. "Aren't you going to answer that?"

"I'm debating."

"There's nothing to debate. We've been an awfully long time," she said, pulling free of his embrace. "Let's hope it's your clothes and not Eric."

It was clothing. After signing for the package, he glanced over his shoulder at her. "With any luck, Eric's put the appropriate construction on our delay and is busy inventing an excuse for being in Nevada." He tore open the package and his towel hit the floor. "You might want to get dressed, too."

With a strangled gasp, Nikki snatched up her overnight bag and flew into the bathroom, slamming the door. It took five minutes to calm down enough to dress, and a further five to dab on enough makeup to conceal the ravages of a restless night. Finally, she emerged, dressed in a businesslike fitted gold skirt and blouse, her hair thoroughly brushed and gathered at the base of her neck with a clip.

Jonah took one look at her and shook his head, his mouth settling into a grim line. "Not a chance."

"What's wrong now?" she questioned defensively.

"You look like my secretary, not my wife." He approached, flicking open the first several buttons of her blouse and removing the clip holding her hair. "Unless we're at work, you wear your hair loose."

"Why?"

"We're making a statement, remember, creating an illusion? That illusion is that we're married and can't keep our mitts off each other. When we walk into the dining room, the first thought that I want Eric to have is that we've just made love and then thrown on whatever clothes came to hand in order to join him." He examined her critically. "No jewelry except your wedding band and wear your heels from last night."

"But they're ivory. They don't match—"

"Exactly. We dressed in haste, remember? Come on. Let's go."

Jamming her feet into the shoes he indicated, she snatched up her purse and followed him to the door. They accomplished the ride in the elevator in total silence. Just before the doors slid open, he cupped the back of her head and pulled her close for a quick, hard kiss.

"I hate it when you do that," she protested the minute he released her.

"If you hate it so much, stop clutching my shirt. And when we join Eric, follow my lead. Understand?"

"No."

"Do it anyway. You ready?"

She nodded, dreading the next few minutes. He started toward the restaurant and she caught his arm. "Jonah, wait." She moistened her lips. "Please. Don't...don't hurt him."

His gaze turned wintry. "I think it's too late for that. Don't you? But if it makes you feel any better, I promise I won't give you the chance to hurt him anymore."

With that, he snagged her elbow and led her toward what she suspected would be the most uncomfortable conversation of her life.

CHAPTER FIVE

"WHAT do you mean we're going to Chicago?" Nikki demanded as they entered the airport lobby. "I need to get back to New York."

"And you will," he retorted, joining the short line in front of the first-class passenger check-in counter. "Just as soon as we stop in Chicago and see my parents."

That didn't sound good. "Do we have to?" she asked faintly.

"Yes, we do." He glanced down at her, correctly interpreting her reaction. "Don't worry. I'll do the talking again."

And suffer through the accusatory stares and barbed silences she'd experienced with Eric? Not a chance. "That's what I'm afraid of. Last time you did the talking, I ended up appearing—"

"Heartless? Guilty as sin? A traitor?"

She shot him a sour look. "You do it deliberately, don't you? You twist everything I say to your own advantage."

"I don't have to twist a single thing. You've managed to tangle yourself in this little web of deceit all on your own. I'm just trying to straighten out your mess. If, in the process, you come across as less than sympathetic, it's not my fault."

"Oh, no?" She planted her hands on her hips. "For your information, I wasn't the only one being deceitful last night, *Joe*. Nor would I be in this mess if you hadn't interfered. I had everything all planned."

His eyebrows winged skyward and he made a small noise that sounded suspiciously like a snort. "You call attending the Montagues' ball a plan?"

"Yes." She ticked off her points one by one. "Go to the ball and find a husband. Make a big production out of introducing him at work. Take care of a personal situation. And let Eric down gently. *Gently*!" She glared at him. "Do you even know the meaning of the word 'gentle'? The man I intended to marry would have."

"I see. Adding another player to the drama is supposed to simplify it. Especially someone unfamiliar with both the role and his lines. And a gentle man, no less." His voice dripped sarcasm. "Now there's a contradiction in terms."

She bit down on her lip to halt the impetuous rush of words. She knew when to beat a temporary retreat in order to salvage her pride. And that time had definitely arrived. Besides, their breakfast with Eric had gone precisely as Jonah had predicted and had been every bit the unmitigated disaster she'd feared. Eric had offered the transparent excuse of calling on a potential customer as his reason for being in Nevada. Jonah had repeated the story he'd invented surrounding their engagement and marriage. And she'd sat there gulping coffee and trying to appear madly in love with one brother while avoiding the hurt gaze of the other.

Taking a deep breath, she asked, "What are you going to tell your parents?"

"The truth. It'll make a pleasant change, if nothing else." The ticket window cleared and he crossed to it, dumping their luggage on the scale. "Reroute these through Chicago for a one-night layover," he requested, slapping their airline tickets on the counter. "And what's your first available flight from Chicago to New York on Monday morning?''

"No! I have to get home tonight,'' Nikki protested. "I'm expected."

"Change your plans," he said without a trace of sympathy. "I've had to. There's a bank of phones behind you. I'm sure the incomparable Jan can reschedule your early-morning appointments with one hand tied behind her back."

Realizing further argument would prove futile, she did as he suggested and crossed to the phones. She called her sister first, keeping it light and breezy. "I won't be home until Monday, I'm afraid. My business took longer than expected. And... and I have a surprise for you."

"For me?" her sister asked. "You didn't have to do that."

"I mean... it's not for you precisely. It's—it's something I got for myself. But I hope you'll be pleased."

"What is it?" Krista demanded. "Tell me."

"I can't. I've been a bit impetuous...." Nikki glanced at Jonah's broad back and swallowed. *Very* impetuous might be closer to the truth.

"*You*? Impetuous? I can't believe it."

"Believe it," Nikki retorted. "I'll see you Monday, though I'm not sure when. And I'll bring my surprise with me. You'll love him." She groaned. "*It*. You'll love *it*."

A momentary silence greeted her statement. "Oh, Nikki," Krista said in a troubled voice. "What have you done?"

"Something wonderful," Nikki insisted with a hint of defiance. She shut her eyes. Wonderfully terrifying. Terrifyingly wonderful. "I'll see you tomorrow."

"And we'll talk, right?"

Nikki winced. "Right. All my love to you and Keli. I've got to run."

"Nick, honey?"

"What?"

"It's not your fault." Krista's voice dropped, the words tumbling out in an urgent rush. "You don't have to spend the rest of your life making up for one youthful indiscretion. You have to stop blaming yourself for what happened. It isn't worth ruining your life over—"

"I'm not," Nikki interrupted briskly. "I'm just trying to take care of you and Keli. It'll work out, I promise."

"Try taking care of yourself for a change," Krista shot back. "That's all I ask."

"I will." Eventually. Just as soon as she'd secured the futures of her various family members.

"Yeah, right." A sigh drifted across the line. "I love you, sweetie."

"Me, too. I'll talk to you soon."

The tears pricking Nikki's eyes caught her by surprise and it took a full minute to collect herself enough to place the next call. Despite being disturbed at home on a Sunday, Jan took the instructions to rearrange Monday's schedule with her customary composure. Just as Nikki concluded the phone call, Jonah approached.

"Finished?"

"All set."

"Good. We'll have to hustle. The flight leaves in fifteen minutes."

"But…aren't you going to call your parents and warn them we're coming?" she asked in dismay.

"I'll do it on the plane. Let's go."

The flight lasted a torturous three hours, giving Nikki ample time for reflection—although she spent most of that time worrying rather than reflecting. She'd met

Loren Sanders when she'd first been hired and only once or twice since. Though he seemed charming, she'd sensed he didn't suffer fools gladly. On the other hand, she'd never met Jonah's mother and knew little of her except what could be gleaned from office gossip. Stories of Della's immense charm and appeal circulated there on a regular basis. Which might be why the idea of confronting the Sanderses with her idiocy was sufficient to put Nikki in a total panic. For she knew without a doubt that that's how she'd be perceived—as an absolute idiot.

Jonah was right. She'd made a mess of this entire situation. She should have forced Eric to listen from the beginning. Instead, she'd compounded deceit with deceit until she'd compromised herself so thoroughly, it was a wonder Jonah didn't just let her choke on all the lies. But then, as he'd so nastily pointed out, if it hadn't been for the potential harm to International Investment's reputation, as well as her nomination for the Lawrence J. Bauman Award, he would have left her to her fate without a single qualm.

At least he couldn't fault her business decisions, she attempted to console herself. Despite what he'd threatened, when he examined her record, he'd be impressed. Very impressed. And on that note, she shut her eyes and willed herself to catch up on some vitally needed sleep.

Jonah glanced at his wife. The instant she'd nodded off, she'd snuggled into his arms as though she belonged. With her head tucked into the curve of his shoulder and her fingers laced through two of his belt loops, it would be understandable for a stranger to think theirs a familiar position.

He should find it humorous, and he might have if not for one troubling detail. Even in sleep, her features had

a drawn appearance he didn't like. He knew it was due
to stress combined with exhaustion. Faint purple bruises
beneath her eyes emphasized her pallor and a tiny line
remained between her brows as though even in her
dreams she hadn't found surcease from her difficulties.

He smoothed his thumb across the bothersome
wrinkle, pleased when he succeeded in ironing it away.
At his touch, she sighed and relaxed more fully against
him.

"Excuse me, Mr. Alexander," the flight attendant
paused to whisper. "We'll be landing shortly. Can I bring
you and your wife some coffee?"

"Thanks," he said with a nod. "Black for me. Two
cups with extra sugar for my wife."

He didn't bother to waken her. The rousing aroma of
the coffee did it for him. She stirred, her nose twitching
first, followed by the reluctant flickering of her lashes.
"Tell me I'm not dreaming," she murmured sleepily.
"Is that really coffee?"

"You don't even have to open your eyes. Just hold
out a hand and it's all yours."

To his amusement, she did as he suggested. Halfway
through her second cup, she straightened. From the flush
tinting her cheeks, he gathered she was somewhat em-
barrassed to have awakened in his arms. And from the
tightening of her mouth, he guessed she intended to
pretend it hadn't happened. Unwilling to allow the ep-
isode to pass without consequence, he reached over and
combed his fingers through the spill of russet hair caressing her cheek. If he'd hoped to disconcert her, it
backfired. Badly. He'd heard of hair being compared to
silk and always thought it a poetic exaggeration. Now
he knew differently. Never had he touched anything so
smooth and soft.

"Feel better?" he asked quietly, tucking the wayward strands behind her ear.

"Yes, thank you." She continued to avoid his gaze. "How much longer until we get there?"

"Fifteen or twenty minutes."

The faint line he'd smoothed away earlier reappeared. "We'll go directly to your parents' house?"

"It's an apartment, and yes, we'll go straight there. I don't expect the traffic to be too bad on a Sunday. It shouldn't take more than forty minutes."

"Oh." She moistened her lips, clearly working up the nerve to ask the question she'd been fretting about for the past five hours. "You said you were going to tell them the truth. What exactly do you plan to say?"

"That Eric's made an ass of himself. That you overreacted. And that if I'd had enough sleep before wading into the middle of things, I would have resolved matters with more finesse than I have."

She shot him a look of alarm. "You think marrying was a mistake, don't you?"

"It was an extreme solution to a not-so-extreme problem. Don't worry. I'll deal with it."

A troubled expression darkened her eyes. "I didn't marry just because of Eric, remember? I do have a secondary reason."

"So you said. Care to tell me about it now?" Her lashes swept downward, but not before he'd caught a telltale flash of violet. Whatever this reason involved, it visibly upset her. And for some reason, she didn't trust him enough yet to explain the details.

"I'd rather wait, if you don't mind," she replied. "It's—"

"Personal. Yes, I know." He lifted an eyebrow. "I hope you're not going to make me guess. With your propensity for chaos, I doubt my imagination is up to the job."

"I'll tell you—" her mouth firmed "—when I'm ready."

"I hope so. I may have difficulty resolving it otherwise."

"I don't want you to resolve it!" she retorted, stung. "I can take care of my own problems."

"So I've noticed." He cut her off before she could say more. "Fasten your seat belt. We're about to land."

By the time they'd collected their luggage and caught a cab to the Sanderses' apartment, the afternoon had all but vanished. Della answered the door to his knock, flinging her arms around him with customary enthusiasm.

"I'm so glad you're here. Dinner will be ready in half an hour, so there's plenty of time to freshen up." She smiled at Nikki and held out her hand, a slight reserve curbing her enthusiasm. "You must be Mrs. Ashton. Welcome."

"It's Nikki," Jonah interrupted lazily. "Nikki Alexander, to be exact. As in Mrs. Jonah Alexander."

"Oh, that just tears it!" Nikki turned on him, her taut control dissolving in the face of her fury.

As he'd hoped, the cool, reserved businesswoman vanished, replaced by an impassioned spitfire. He found the spitfire much more to his liking. Knowing his parents, they would, too. "Something wrong?" he asked innocently.

"You—you need to ask?" she sputtered. "You couldn't have broken the news to your mother more gently?"

"I don't do gentle, remember?"

Della's mouth fell open. "You're *married*?"

Nikki planted her hands on her trim hips, her fury a glorious sight. At least Jonah found it glorious. He slanted a quick look at his mother, relieved that she appeared more confused than shocked.

"It didn't occur to you to prepare her first instead of just nuking everyone in sight with your announcement?" Nikki demanded.

He shrugged, fighting to keep a straight face. "Don't exaggerate. The only everyone in sight is my mother. And I prefer speed to delicacy."

"Well, that's obvious." She shot him a reproving glance. "Although in your line of work, I'd have thought you'd have learned something about diplomacy."

"Not much," he confessed. "I've always found making money takes talent and intelligence, not tact."

Della glanced over her shoulder. "Loren, you better get out here."

Nikki's eyes glittered with ill-humor, the color as vivid as a tropical sunrise. "That's beside the point. You told me you were going to call them."

"I did call—while you were asleep." She sounded a bit grouchy, Jonah decided. Perhaps he should have fed her three cups of coffee instead of just two. "I told them we were coming for dinner."

"What's all the yelling about?" Loren questioned mildly as he joined his wife.

"That's it? Just 'we're coming for dinner'?" Nikki stabbed a finger at Jonah. "You couldn't have added, 'And by the way, Nikki Ashton and I just got married. I'll explain when we get there'?"

"They're married," Della announced to her husband. "Jonah and Nikki."

"How can they be married?" Loren demanded. "She's already married to that Ashton fellow."

"See? This is why I waited." Jonah leaned against the doorjamb, confiding, "Getting married is the sort of happy news parents prefer to hear face-to-face."

"In the *hallway*?" Nikki questioned, infuriated.

"They want to share in our joy and happiness, no matter where we are."

"They don't look the least joyful or happy. They look...stunned."

"I'm not stunned. I'm confused," Loren grumbled to his wife. "I thought she was having an affair with Eric."

Della shrugged. "Well, now she's married to Jonah."

"You couldn't even wait until we were invited in?" Nikki folded her arms across her chest and glared at Jonah. "Maybe work it casually into the conversation over drinks?"

He fought to assume an appropriately contrite expression. "I must have gotten carried away in the excitement of the moment. It just came out."

"You, carried away?" She snorted. "My Aunt Fanny. You never do anything without a reason."

Loren looked from one to the other, his brow wrinkling. "Who the hell is Aunt Fanny? And while we're on the subject of relatives...what the dickens happened to Mr. Ashton? Have we ever figured that one out?"

"There is no Mr. Ashton," Nikki and Jonah said in unison.

Loren thrust a hand through his salt-and-pepper hair. "No Mr. Ashton? I don't understand any of this. Would someone please tell me what the devil is going on around here?"

"Maybe we should finish this discussion inside before the neighbors complain," Della suggested.

"Excellent suggestion, Mother," Jonah approved.

An awkward moment followed while they all filed from the entranceway into the living room. "What a gorgeous view," Nikki volunteered.

Della offered a strained smile. "You should see it when it snows."

"Yes, yes. The view is wonderful. Snow is wonderful. The whole damned world is just by golly wonderful!" Loren declared testily. "Now what the hell is going on here? Or is a reasonable explanation too much to expect?"

"It's all my fault," Nikki began.

"I believe I told you that I'd handle this." Jonah's tone didn't brook defiance.

She lifted her chin. "Fine. You handle it." Turning her back on him, she crossed to stare out at Lake Michigan. What did it matter how he slanted the story? His parents were going to be upset regardless.

"I'll see if I can't keep this simple. There is no Mr. Ashton. Nikki isn't married and never was. She pretended to be married because Eric was making inopportune advances." At Della's muffled exclamation, Jonah shook his head. "No, Mother. It wasn't anything like that. He'd just allowed an understandable infatuation to get the better of his common sense." To his amusement, both Della and Nikki blushed.

Loren's brows drew together. "Let me get this straight. In order to put Eric off, Ms. Ashton—Nikki—invented a marriage?"

"'Fraid so," Jonah confirmed. "And that's when matters got a little out of hand."

"I'd say matters were out of hand a good bit before then," Loren inserted drily.

Jonah exchanged a silent look of agreement with his stepfather. "No comment."

"Could we get on with this?" Nikki pleaded. "I know I screwed up. It's no secret."

Jonah took up the story again. "When Eric continued to express his concern over the prolonged absence of Nikki's husband, she decided to rectify the situation. Last night, she attended a marriage ball in Nevada with the full intention of finding herself a suitable husband to present at work."

Della sank onto the couch. "Oh, my dear child. How could you?"

"It seemed like a good idea at the time," Nikki whispered.

"The suitable husband she found was me." He eyed his parents, his expression implacable. "Until Eric is past this infatuation of his and we get the situation at the New York office straightened out, Nikki and I stay married. And we all treat it as if it were real and permanent."

"Well, I think you have both lost your minds." Loren crossed to the wet bar and poured himself a Scotch. "And I want no part of it."

Jonah glanced at Nikki and his mother. "Give me a minute with him."

Della rose to her feet. "As much as it pains me to say this..." She smiled at Nikki. "Shall we check on dinner?"

"Do we have a choice?"

"I'm afraid not."

Jonah waited until the two women were out of earshot, then turned to confront his stepfather. "Whether you agree with my decision or not, I expect your support on this. And I expect you to treat Nikki with all the respect due my wife. If you can't, tell me now and we'll leave."

Loren's brows shot up. "You're serious?"

"Very. You called me home to take care of a situation, and that's what I'm doing."

"It's how you're taking care of it that worries me."

"Blame it on jet lag."

For the first time, a hint of amusement touched Loren's face. "I thought you didn't believe in jet lag," he said, pouring his stepson a drink.

"I do now," Jonah replied wryly.

"But marriage?" The older man shook his head. "You don't really expect me to endorse such a crazy scheme?"

"Look, Loren, we have to protect International Investment at all costs, which means we can't fire her, and for the time being, we can't transfer her."

"So, what do you propose?"

"Just this…" Jonah took a healthy swallow of Scotch. "The LJB Award comes right before Christmas, so we hang tough till then. I have an excellent assistant in London who can take care of our overseas operation until after the holidays. In the meantime, I'll spend the next six weeks in New York playing the doting husband."

Loren shot his stepson a shrewd look. "What will you really be doing?"

"Looking over Nikki's track record and making sure she and Eric haven't screwed up any other accounts. As soon as I feel matters are under control, I'll return to London. We give it six more months after that. Then we encourage the lovely Ms. Ashton to either transfer far from Eric's sphere of influence or find employment elsewhere."

Loren lifted an eyebrow. "Your solution is a bit rough on your wife, isn't it?"

Anger lit Jonah's eyes. "My wife is directly responsible for this situation with Eric. If she'd told him no, or contacted any one of us when it became a problem, we wouldn't be in our current mess."

"What happens once the situation with Eric is resolved?" Loren asked.

"Nikki and I divorce," he stated baldly.

"Divorce? Don't you mean get an annulment?"

Jonah's mouth tugged to one side. "I believe that falls under the heading of none of your business."

"Perhaps. But she is my employee. Come to think of it, she's also my stepdaughter-in-law. At least for the time being."

"Point taken." Jonah finished off the Scotch and set the glass gently on the bar. "When the time comes, we'll divorce."

"This time, I'm doing the talking," Nikki stated firmly. At least she stated it as firmly as she could, considering Jonah's uncanny ability to get his own way. She found the knack quite disconcerting and suspected that not only did he know it, he took advantage of that fact.

"We'll see," he replied in a noncommittal voice. The cab pulled up in front of an attractive brownstone and he peered at it through the smudged passenger window. "Is this it?"

"Yes. I rent out the first floor and we occupy the second."

"We?"

"My...my sister, Krista, and her daughter, Keli. They live with me."

"Their picture is the one in your office?"

"How...?" Her eyes narrowed. "Oh, that's right. You searched my desk. Yes, that's Krista and Keli. The photo was taken last year when Keli was five."

Jonah unloaded the luggage and paid off the driver. "How long have you lived here?" he asked as they climbed the steps to the front door.

"Forever." Her response sounded short to the point of rudeness, but she was reluctant to trust him with even such a small piece of her privacy. "Krista and I grew up here."

He paused at the top of the landing. "I assume you haven't told her about us."

"No." She caught her bottom lip between her teeth. "And fair warning, she may not take the news too well."

"No problem," he responded drily. "I'm getting used to that sort of response to our announcement. Is she the other reason for your decision to marry?"

"Yes." Taking a deep breath, she admitted, "I guess I should have explained earlier."

"That might have helped," he agreed blandly. "Although now works just as well for me. Does Krista know your first marriage was a fake?"

"Yes, but she's not to know this one is, too." Alarm flickered in her gaze. "Which reminds me, don't, under any circumstances, tell her you're related to Eric or she'll know for sure something's up."

His eyebrow notched upward. "I take it this is supposed to be a love match?"

"Yes, yes," she said with a nervous glance at the door. "We're in love. Madly, passionately in love."

"Got it." He tilted his head to one side. "Care to tell me why we're madly, passionately et cetera, et cetera? What are we trying to accomplish?"

"You don't need to know that. You just have to act the part of the love-struck groom." Impatience edged her voice. "Can you do it?"

"In spades."

Without warning, he wrapped powerful arms around her and yanked her against a granite-hard expanse of chest. Before she could catch her breath to protest, he nailed her with an all-consuming kiss. She should struggle came the dazed thought. She should give him hell. She should level him with a good, swift kick to the shins. Instead, she wrapped her arms around his neck and gave herself up to the illicit thrill of the embrace, only vaguely aware of his fumbling for something behind her. It took a moment to realize he was leaning on the doorbell. By the time it dawned on her, the door had been flung open.

"Aunt Nikki!" a childish voice declared. "You're home. I've been waiting and waiting— Oh!"

"Jonah!" Nikki whispered frantically, shoving at his massive shoulders. "Let go."

The little girl began to giggle. "Mommy! Come quick! There's a strange man kissing Aunt Nikki."

"My goodness! So there is." Another voice had joined the party.

Nikki managed to wriggle free of Jonah's hold. Turning, she offered her sister a flustered smile, then had the breath knocked out of her as the child launched herself at her aunt for an exuberant hug.

"What's your surprise?" Keli demanded, wrapping her arms around her aunt's waist.

"I think that's me," Jonah confessed, lowering himself to her level. "You must be Keli. I'm your Uncle Jonah."

Nikki watched as her niece peeped shyly up at him. Even in a crouch, Jonah's impressive size tended to overwhelm, and Keli studied him uncertainly for a long moment. Wisps of strawberry blond curls floated in a brilliant halo around her face, highlighting the doubt written all over her dainty features. Then, like a shadow floating clear of the sun, the doubt vanished and she grinned.

"Hi," she said. "I didn't know I had an uncle."

"Neither did I," Krista said in a confused voice. She offered a hand to Jonah as he stood. "I'm Krista Barrett, Nikki's sister. And you are...?" She lifted a winged eyebrow.

"Jonah Alexander," he said, accepting her hand. "Your brother-in-law."

"Oh, good heavens!"

"We are *not* doing this on the doorstep again," Nikki interjected.

He grinned. "I believe we just did."

"Everyone inside," Nikki snapped. "We'll talk there."

With a shrug, Jonah picked up the bags and stepped across the threshold. Keli trotted after him, studying her new uncle with unabashed curiosity.

Krista caught Nikki's arm as she started past. "What's going on?" she demanded softly.

"I'm married."

"For real this time?" Krista questioned, not bothering to conceal her concern. "This isn't another scheme you've dreamed up because of that Eric Sanders?"

"The marriage is real enough." Nikki took a deep breath and fought to put as much conviction and enthusiasm in her voice as possible. "And just so you know, I love him. In fact, we're both madly in love. And it's permanent. 'Til death us do part and all that."

Krista's brows drew together. "Uh-huh."

"I mean it!"

Nikki sent Jonah an uneasy glance. He stood with Keli, listening to her excited chatter. "And this is the living room," the child was explaining earnestly. "We keep it all picked up for Aunt Nikki. She works real hard and it helps her when I keep my toys in our bedroom."

"The one you share with your mom?" he asked.

"How'd you know that?"

"A lucky guess." An odd expression had crept into his gaze, Nikki realized with a tinge of apprehension. They'd taken on that autumn chill again, the brown-gold appearing rock hard.

"Well," Krista said in bewilderment, "I guess congratulations are in order. I'm sure we have a bottle of champagne around here someplace." She stared at Jonah. "Your name is familiar. Do I know you from somewhere? Do you live nearby?"

"No, you don't and no, he doesn't," Nikki answered with more haste than grace. "He's just come back from overseas. He doesn't have anyplace to live, which means he'll be moving in with us."

"That's going to make it a bit crowded," Krista observed, then offered, "Why don't I put out some feelers to some of my friends? I'm sure I could find another place."

Nikki wrinkled her brow in what she hoped was a thoughtful frown. "That's a possibility. But there's no hurry."

"No hurry at all," Jonah cut in coldly. "In fact, we want you and Keli to stay put. We'll be moving into my apartment."

Nikki's mouth fell open. "But—"

"I was keeping it as a surprise wedding gift, sweetheart. Krista, the place is all yours," Jonah stated in an intractable voice. "We just stopped by to give you the good news and to pick up some of Nikki's clothes." His hand clamped down on her arm as she started to protest. "Didn't we?"

"I'm so pleased you let me do the talking," she bit out, watching all her plans dissipate like smoke in a high wind. Aware of Krista's worried stare, she added a terse, "Darling."

"My pleasure." He bared sharklike teeth. "Honey."

CHAPTER SIX

"How could you?" Nikki demanded furiously.

"How could I? How could *you*?"

"You don't understand!"

"You're damned right I don't," Jonah snarled, tossing their luggage into the spacious elevator. Inserting a key in the floor-selector panel, he slammed his palm against the button for the penthouse. "Krista is a member of your family. Doesn't that mean anything to you?"

"Of course it does—"

"And yet you'd still toss your own sister and niece out of their home?"

He swiveled to confront her, and the spaciousness of the car instantly shrank. She felt as though she'd stumbled into a lion's den and found herself face-to-face with the top cat—a savage, ill-tempered beast only too happy to shred some flesh from her bones. It wasn't a pleasant sensation.

"I'd never force Krista to leave," she insisted.

"But you'd make it so uncomfortable for her, she'd vacate of her own accord, right?" The contempt in his voice ripped at her self-control. "I'll bet it's the only home those two have ever known, isn't it?"

She didn't dare answer that one, not when her response would further incite him. "Krista doesn't want to live with me anymore," Nikki attempted to explain. "She wants to move in with a friend. I'm just trying to give her a gracious way out."

His eyes flashed with gold fire. "Oh, you're giving her a gracious way out, all right. Right out the door and onto the street."

"That's not true! The problem is, she won't leave because she doesn't want me to live alone. She's got this crazy idea that she owes me."

He folded his arms across his chest, drawing her attention to the imposing width of his shoulders. Where once she took comfort in his size, now it only served to intimidate. "And who gave her that idea? You?"

She wouldn't explain, and no amount of baiting on his part could force her to. "I don't care what you think," she said tightly. "I told you from the start that I needed a husband in order to resolve two problems."

"Eric and a personal matter. I remember." He speared her with a flinty look. "If I'd had any idea what that personal matter involved or how you planned to rectify it, I'd never have married you."

"And if I'd known you'd end up interfering in something that's none of your business, I wouldn't have married you, either," she flashed back, her temper smoldering. "Krista and Keli are the two most important people in my life—"

He gave a short, hard laugh. "You have a funny way of showing it."

"I let you handle Eric the way you thought best. But you didn't grant me the same courtesy, did you?"

"There's one important difference. I had Eric's best interests at heart."

"Just as I had Krista's! If you'd let me do the talking instead of butting in the way you did, it would have all worked out fine. But now you've ruined everything I worked so hard to arrange. I went to all the expense and awkwardness of marrying for nothing. *Nothing!* And it's all your fault."

He turned to stare at the elevator doors, the muscles of his jaw flexing. "Fine. It's all my fault. I can live with that."

Fury exploded to life with all the force of a wildfire. She fought to control the rage, to dampen it with cool, calming logic and reason. For the first time in recent memory, she couldn't. "You had no right to interfere! None. I'd planned it so carefully, taken away every last excuse she could dream up. And thanks to you, my plans are ruined."

"You think I give a damn about that?" He turned sharply to face her. "Don't expect me to apologize for protecting Krista and Keli from your machinations. I'm glad I interfered."

"You don't understand." She closed her eyes to hide her frustration. Because of Jonah, Krista wouldn't be moving out anytime soon. That was quite clear. Why fly the nest when it was so convenient and safe to remain? Why risk the pain and sorrow of a cruel world when she could use Nikki as the perfect excuse for staying put? Nikki needed her. She owed Nikki. Nikki had saved her life. "Now she'll never leave."

"Tough."

"Tough?" She stared at him in disbelief. "What am I supposed to do when our marriage ends? I can't move back in with Krista. She'll never get on with her life if I do."

"All I've done is prevent you from throwing your sister and niece onto the street." The elevator doors slid open and once again he picked up the luggage, transferring it to the door of the penthouse. "Why not let your sister continue to use the brownstone? Kids should have a house to call their own. When we divorce, you can find an apartment. Something immaculate where you won't have to worry about a kid cluttering up your space with her toys.''

''You still don't understand,'' she repeated.

''You're right. I don't.'' He keyed open the door and swept her into his arms.

''What are you doing?'' she demanded in alarm.

''Carrying my bride over the threshold. Welcome home, Mrs. Alexander.'' Then he dumped her onto her feet. ''Don't get too comfortable.''

Nikki blinked hard, fighting the unexpected rush of tears. Turning away so he wouldn't see how much he'd upset her, she crossed the black marble entryway into the living room. A bank of windows lined one wall, offering a stunning panorama of Manhattan. It was clearly the focal point of the room. The furniture had been artfully arranged to take advantage of the view while still maintaining an air of intimacy. It was beautiful and expensive and chillingly cold.

''It must have been pricey maintaining this place while you were in England,'' she commented without turning around. Though she hadn't heard him enter the room, the shiver that slid down her spine gave her all the warning she needed.

''It's not mine. International Investment uses it for entertaining,'' he replied. ''Or we'll allow the occasional client to stay here when he or she flies in from out of town.''

''Won't Della and Loren object to our using it?''

''It's my decision. Why would they object?''

She turned around, regarding him curiously. ''Isn't it Loren's call? Isn't he the CEO?''

''Don't you know?''

"Know what?"

"I'm CEO. It's a recent change, I'll admit. But still, a woman in your position should have made it her business to stay current."

"Eric never said and I assumed..." She shrugged. "My mistake."

"One of many, it would seem."

She refused to allow him to get under her skin again. "So what now?"

"Now we have lunch and then go to work. I expect Eric will have gone in bright and early this morning and leaked the news of our marriage. Once there, we introduce you as Mrs. Alexander. We accept the employees' congratulations, ignore their curious whispers and stares and get down to business."

"What about after we make the big announcement?" she asked. "I mean, what happens when you return to England?"

"I don't go back until some time after the holidays. We'll have plenty of opportunity to discuss our options."

Her eyes narrowed. "Why so long? At the Montagues', you claimed you'd only be in the country for a few weeks."

"My plans changed when we married."

"Why?" she repeated baldly.

"It would look strange if your husband missed out on your big night." At her blank look, he prompted, "You know. The LJB Award."

With all the furor of the past several days, she'd forgotten about the award ceremony. But Jonah hadn't. And with sudden, devastating insight she realized that her nomination must have played an important part in his choosing to marry her when Eric made his unexpected appearance. "It wouldn't do for International

Investment to lose an LJB nominee, would it?" she asked.

"I prefer not to."

"But if the nominee isn't a winner? What then?"

He tilted his head to one side. "I'm not certain," he admitted frankly. "I'd like to see the quality of your work before I reach that decision."

"You won't be disappointed," she informed him confidently. "I'm good at what I do."

He didn't appear convinced. "We'll see."

Krista hesitated in front of the reception desk of International Investment, not quite certain whether she had to check in before going in search of Nikki's office. But since the desk wasn't occupied, she couldn't ask for either directions or instructions.

She'd never bothered her sister at work before, but the past three weeks had been odd. Something wasn't right. The few times she'd been over to Nikki's new apartment, there hadn't been an opportunity for private conversation. So she'd decided to hold the discussion here. Noticing a small crowd clustered near a huge double door at the far end of the hallway, she decided to ask one of them for directions.

"Excuse me," she began, tapping the shoulder of a tall man with golden brown hair.

"Sshh." He waved her silent without turning around. "This is too good to miss."

"What—" And then she heard it—shouting coming from the far side of the door. Her eyes widened. Good gracious, that sounded like...

Nikki.

"What do you mean you've reassigned the Stamberg account?" her always-in-control, emotions-on-ice sister shrieked. "That's my account!"

"Well, now it's Meyerson's," a masculine voice roared back. Krista's mouth dropped open. If she wasn't mistaken, that sounded very much like the brother-in-law she'd gained three weeks ago. Her brow wrinkled in confusion. She hadn't realized he worked with Nikki.

"Meyerson? That idiot? He can't tell a put from a place, much less organize a portfolio as complicated as Stamberg's. I thought you wanted to improve business."

"I do."

"Well, guess what? This isn't going to do it."

"You seem to forget who's working for whom around here," Jonah snarled.

"I doubt that will be a problem much longer."

"And just what the hell does that mean?"

"It means that a few more asinine decisions like this one and you won't have to worry about impertinent employees, portfolios, accounts, or who's working for whom at International. Because we'll all be out of work!"

"You don't know what the hell you're talking about."

"I know one thing. Appointing Meyerson is the biggest mistake you'll ever make."

"Meyerson will double Stamberg's profits."

"Don't make me laugh. Meyerson couldn't double his own age."

"Shall we make a small wager about that? Or are you all talk and no action?"

"You want action? I'll give you action. Not only won't Meyerson double so much as one of Stamberg's stock picks, but he'll lose money on the few investments he does make."

"And if you're wrong?"

"Then I'll... I'll..."

"You'll what?"

"I'll dance naked on top of your desk!" Krista heard her sister declare rashly. "But if you lose, you do the honors on top of mine."

A collective gasp rippled through the crowd, and Krista leaned against the wall, torn between shock and amusement. This was a side of Nikki she'd never heard before.

"What I wouldn't give to see that," one of the men muttered.

"Shut up, Bently," the man she'd first approached growled.

"Oh, dear, oh, dear," a balding man groaned. "What will I do?"

"You'd better win that bet, Meyerson, or Alexander will have your head on a platter," Bently warned.

There'd been several minutes of silence behind the door. Then Krista heard the sound of a chair being shoved back. "You've got yourself a deal," Jonah said. "Prepare to lose, wife."

"Hah! There's not a chance in hell you'll win this bet."

Her voice grew louder as she approached the door and everyone hastily dispersed. The man who'd told Bently to shut up turned, catching her off guard. "Don't just stand there," he said, grasping Krista's arm. He thrust open the nearest door and practically shoved her over the threshold. "Nikki won't appreciate our eaves-dropping on her conversation."

He crowded in behind her and Krista found it difficult to breathe. He couldn't be aware he still held her, she decided, closing her eyes against the unexpected warmth

pooling in her stomach. Or that he'd molded her so
tightly against his lean form. Feelings she hadn't experienced in almost seven long, lonely years stirred, disconcerting her. "Please—" she began.

"Wait a sec," he murmured close to her ear. Opening
the door a crack, he glanced into the hallway. "Here she
comes."

"Oh, really?" Nikki was saying, fury rippling through
her voice. "Well, we'll just see about that." A door
opened and then slammed closed. She swept by, rich
color blooming in her face. Never had she looked so
alive, or so beautiful, Krista thought.

The door opened once again and she caught a glimpse
of Jonah. "Yes, we will see. And in the meantime,
prepare to start stripping!" The door slamming punctuated his final taunt.

Krista wriggled. "If you don't mind," she said.

"Oh, sorry." He stepped back, his hands falling slowly
away. Gazing down at her, he frowned. "You look familiar. Do I know you?"

"I don't think so." She held out her hand and gave
a rueful smile. "I'm Krista Barrett. Nikki's my sister."

He blinked in surprise, then began to chuckle. "No
kidding. I'm Eric Sanders. Jonah's my brother."

Startled, she stared at him. This was the man who'd
been infatuated with Nikki? The man who'd made her
so uncomfortable she'd invented a husband? *And* he was
the brother of Nikki's new husband? Something strange
was going on here. This had to be more than a coinci-
dence. Which meant that Nikki's marriage might not be
a simple love match as her dear sister had claimed. Krista
eyed Eric speculatively. Maybe he knew what was up.
And maybe, just maybe, he'd clue her in.

"Listen, I know this is a bit unexpected, but... would you care to have lunch with me?" Eric offered.

"I don't know," she said. "I'd hoped to see Nikki."

He grinned, a charming, boyish sort of grin. "I don't think this is a very good time to talk to her, do you?"

"I guess not." She studied him, finding his gentle appeal impossible to resist. Besides, lunch might be the perfect opportunity to pump him for a little information. "Okay. Let's go."

"Great." Warmth gathered in his hazel eyes along with something else.... Masculine appreciation, she finally discerned with bemused astonishment. It had been so long since she'd experienced it, she almost hadn't recognized that sudden, explosive attraction. He reached for the doorknob, then hesitated. "I guess I should tell you that I used to be very attracted to your sister. Nothing happened, you understand," he added hastily.

She hid her amusement. "I understand."

"Besides, I just realized something."

"What did you realize?"

"That while Nikki's perfect for Jonah, she'd have been a bit much for me. Besides, she's a career woman and I'd really like a more traditional wife." A slow smile lit his gaze and he opened the door. "So tell me, Krista. How do you like children?"

She laughed. "Funny you should ask."

Nikki entered her office and banged the door closed behind her. Never in the twenty-eight years of her existence had she been so furious. And it was all due to one infuriating, impossible man.

Her husband.

She paced the office, trying to calm herself, struggling to regain control. It didn't work. Nothing worked—not staring out the window and counting cabs, not reorganizing her well-organized files, not even tidying her already-tidy desk. Only one thing would calm her. Grimly, she crossed to her office closet and dragged out a large carton. After removing a huge tarp from the top of the box, she spread it on the floor. It was followed by a whole array of equipment—a special blend of soil, fertilizer, gloves, snippers, atomizer, an assortment of ceramic pots and an apron. She laid everything out with military precision, then crossed to the window to gather up her plants.

They'd been given to her by various staff members, all of whom had one thing in common—black thumbs. She took pleasure in nursing the plants back to full health before returning them. As always when she worked with her plants, the fury of her emotions eased, dissipating until she was once again in control. She worked straight through lunch, happily repotting.

An hour later, she finished. Feeling much more relaxed, she rocked back on her heels and tossed her gloves onto the tarp. She nodded in satisfaction as she gathered up her supplies. Two of her specimens could be returned by the end of the week, she decided. And undoubtedly, there'd be several others to replace the ones she gave back. She made a mental note to sweep the office for more casualties. With Christmas fast approaching, she didn't doubt she'd be kept quite busy. Just as she finished cleaning up the clutter, the phone rang.

"Nikki Ashton," she said without thinking, then made a face. "I mean, Alexander."

"Nikki, dear. It's Selma."

"Hello, Aunt Selma." She tucked a strand of hair behind her ear and smiled in genuine pleasure. "How are you?"

"Wonderful. Excited. In urgent need of advice."

Nikki brightened. "You know I'm happy to help."

"I know you are, dear. That's why we always call on you."

"So what's up?"

"Ernie and I have had the most delicious offer." Excitement bubbled in her voice. "Of course, we want to discuss it with you before we act."

Some of Nikki's pleasure faded. This didn't sound good. But then, Selma and Ernie's ideas seldom did. "Why don't you drop by the office tomorrow? Is noon convenient?"

"No, no. It has to be tonight. We're much too excited to wait any longer. Besides, time is of the essence. We'll come to your place."

Nikki straightened abruptly. "I don't think—"

"Krista says your apartment is gorgeous and we'd love to meet that new husband of yours. Shame on you for eloping, by the way, and doing us out of the pleasure of a big wedding." There was a delicate pause and then Selma asked, "What time, dear?"

Nikki thought fast. "How about six?" she suggested, unable to dream up a reasonable excuse for changing the venue.

"Six it is. See you then."

Hanging up, Nikki leaned back in her chair. It would work out, she attempted to reassure herself. With any luck, Jonah would work as late tonight as he had every other evening this week and she could meet her relatives without his interference. At least he'd better not interfere. Not again. Not when Aunt Selma and Uncle Ernie required such delicate handling.

She closed her eyes, tension creeping back. Maybe she'd better sweep the office for more plants right now. Why repot tomorrow when she could repot today?

"All we need to do is put up fifty thousand and we'll have the exclusive franchise," Selma said, clasping her hands together enthusiastically.

"But it's a limited-time offer," Ernie added. "If we don't get the money together by the day after tomorrow, we're going to miss the boat."

"This is one boat it wouldn't be such a bad idea to miss," Nikki muttered beneath her breath.

"What's that, dear?" Selma asked anxiously.

"A note. I didn't want to miss making a note of the date. The day after tomorrow," she repeated, writing Wednesday in large block letters. "And what's the name of this man who wants you to invest?"

"Timothy T. Tucker. Such a delightful man, isn't he, Ernie?"

"Really knows his way around numbers. Had our heads spinning. Why the way he has it figured, we can triple our investment in under a year."

Nikki tossed down her pen. "Uncle Ernie, even I can't do that."

He patted her hand. "Yes, sweetheart. We know. But we won't hold that against you."

"You do your best, I'm sure," Selma maintained stoutly. "We're all very proud of you."

Nikki groaned. "How did you meet this man? What do you know about him?"

"He walked into our coffee shop right out of the blue."

"A red-letter day that was," Ernie pronounced, folding his hands over his ample middle. "Looked around and knew right off we ran a profitable business."

"I'll just bet." Nikki scowled. He'd probably watched the flow of traffic, made a few quick calculations and decided the shop kicked off plenty of disposable income. Then he'd have asked a few questions of her naive aunt and uncle and...*voilà*. The birth of a scam. "Did you tell him about your mortgage?"

Selma looked surprised. "But we don't have one, dear."

"I know that, Aunt Selma. Does this Mr. Tucker know? Did you tell him?"

"I think we may have touched on it," Selma confessed. "But it was all very innocent. He was interested in opening a storefront in our area and wondered what the rent might run."

"Of course we had to admit we didn't know," Uncle Ernie inserted. "Since we own the property outright, we aren't all that knowledgeable about what rents go for these days."

"Why, if he's selling these franchises, does he need to rent a storefront?" Nikki questioned in exasperation.

"To interest people in buying the Miracle Box, of course."

"But that doesn't make any sense." Unfortunately, her aunt and uncle put little credence in logic and reason, much less common sense. "If you have the franchise to sell this box, why would *he* open—"

Selma reached over and patted her hand. "Don't feel bad, darling. We were confused at first, too. Dear Mr. Tucker was so patient with us, though. Wasn't he, Ernie?"

"Answered every one of our questions. Explained about the patents and our territory and made all that technical jargon sound quite sensible." He grinned proudly. "Why, I can talk about fax modules and cable companions with the best of them."

"So I see." Picking up her pen and pulling her steno pad closer, Nikki started jotting down notes. "Timothy T. Tucker. The Miracle Box. Fifty grand. Wednesday. I don't suppose you have his business card by any chance?"

"Sure." Ernie plucked it from his wallet and handed it over. "Must be doing all right for himself. Cards of that quality are expensive."

"I wonder where he gets all that wealth?" Nikki asked, not the least surprised when they didn't pick up on her sarcasm.

"From ideas like the Miracle Box, I imagine," Ernie said thoughtfully.

"And how are you going to sell these boxes and still run your coffee shop?"

"Gordie and Cal are helping."

Nikki closed her eyes and sighed. She should have known her cousins would be involved. If it was an idiotic scheme and sure to cost a lot of money with little to no return, they'd be the first in line. Her aunt and uncle would be second.

"So what do you think?" Ernie asked anxiously. "May we have the money?"

"Not a chance," Nikki answered without thinking.

"Oh, Nikki. Please. It's not so much to ask. We really need the money, dear." Selma fumbled in her purse for a hankie, applying it to teary eyes. "If you won't do it for us, think of your poor cousins. It's an opportunity that will never come along again."

Nikki groaned. "I couldn't be so lucky."

"We have a CD coming due next week," Ernie reminded her. "Can't we borrow against that?"

"I have an investment lined up for that money already."

"What about our savings account?" Selma asked. "Isn't there enough in there?"

Nikki shook her head. "I thought you wanted that money so you could open up Ernie's Beanery 2."

"We can wait. Why, with the money we'll make selling—"

"No."

"But *why*?" Selma dissolved into tears. "I thought it was our money."

"It is," Nikki admitted uncomfortably.

"Then why can't we spend it the way we want?"

"You can," a new voice interrupted. Jonah stepped into the living room. "Can't they, Nikki?"

CHAPTER SEVEN

"NO, THEY can't," Nikki retorted. "Stay out of it, Jonah. You don't understand."

"That doesn't come as any surprise." He tossed his coat and suit jacket over the arm of the couch and deposited his suitcase on the floor beside it. "I seem to have a knack for misunderstanding."

A hint of angry color washed into her cheeks, and her eyes flashed with violet warning. Jonah smiled in satisfaction. He knew what that meant. If he goaded her just a little more, she'd lose her temper as thoroughly as she had earlier that morning. He'd enjoyed their clashes over the past few weeks. He particularly enjoyed shaking her composure, watching as the icy facade melted enough to reveal the vibrant flame within.

"If you don't mind, I'm having a private discussion here."

"But I do mind, sweetheart. You haven't introduced us." Jonah approached and held out his hand, wondering who these people were and why they'd turned their finances over to his wife. "I'm Jonah Alexander, Nikki's husband."

"Ernie and Selma Crandell." They shook hands. "You sure are a busy man. We've been trying to arrange a little get-together ever since Nikki told us you two got married, but you've always had a schedule conflict."

"Is that right? I wish I'd known." Jonah glanced at his wife and said with deceptive mildness, "Sweetheart, you should have nagged me more. If I'd realized that your—" He broke off pointedly.

"Aunt and uncle," she whispered.

A deadly silence descended for an endless moment before Jonah picked up the slack. "If I'd realized your aunt and uncle had been serious about throwing us a party, I would have found the time."

"Well, since we missed out having you for Thanksgiving, perhaps we can make a try for Christmas," Selma offered tentatively. "Or do you have another commitment? Nikki wasn't certain."

Jonah's mouth compressed. Selma clearly wasn't aware that he'd never even heard their names before, let alone received any of their invitations. But Ernie didn't appear quite so obtuse.

"Maybe we've caught you at a bad time," he muttered uncomfortably. "Don't mean to be pushy relatives."

"Not at all." Jonah shot a grim look toward his wife. She made a point of avoiding his gaze, but couldn't hide the guilty color staining her cheekbones. "I'll see if I can't arrange to be free. In fact, I'll make a special note of it on my calendar."

Ernie gave a more enthusiastic nod. "Great. Since we're all the family Nikki and Krista have, we try to make the most of the holidays. My wife and their mom were sisters, you know."

"Were?"

Ernie shot his niece a curious glance. "Did she forget to mention?"

"Apparently, there's quite a bit she forgot to mention," Jonah observed drily.

"Oh. Well, Nikki's mom and dad were killed eight years ago in a boating accident," Ernie explained. "She was just a teenager, poor mite."

"Hardly a teenager or a mite," Nikki corrected crisply, jumping into the conversation. "I was twenty and a very independent college student."

"Eight years ago." Jonah glanced thoughtfully at his wife. She sat in her chair, every muscle tensed. Where only moments ago, her color had run high, she now appeared pale as a winter moon. The urge to protect her from a topic that caused such obvious pain battled with his intense curiosity. He couldn't resist probing just a little deeper. "That would have made Krista..."

"Sixteen," Selma supplied, shaking her head. "That year and a half after their death was such a tragic time. Perhaps if Edward and Angeline had lived, things might have been different for the girls. But with Krista marrying so young and then Nikki involved in that terrible incident—"

"I think that's enough," Nikki interrupted tautly. "I'm sure Jonah doesn't want to hear all the boring details. Besides, it's ancient history."

He pinned her with a narrow gaze. It would seem they'd pushed an emotional hot button. Interesting. "I didn't mean to upset you. We can save this particular conversation for a more convenient time."

Alarm lit her expressive eyes. "There's no need."

If she'd hoped to discourage him, she'd failed. Miserably. Instead, she'd whetted his appetite to learn more. He suspected that whatever had happened seven years ago would shed significant light on several aspects of Nikki's personality—such as the tight control she kept on her emotions. It might also explain her odd attitude toward family.

"She's right," Jonah conceded with an easy smile. "This isn't the appropriate time to talk about the past. I see I've interrupted an important financial discussion." He settled onto the couch and gestured for them to continue. "Please. Don't let me interrupt."

"I believe we've concluded this discussion," Nikki announced, thrusting back her chair.

"But what about the money?" Selma turned to appeal to Jonah. "The deadline's Wednesday."

"I'm certain Nikki won't want to disappoint you," Jonah assured her. "Will you, darling?"

Nikki gathered up her notes, her color riding high once again. "I'll look into it further," she offered through gritted teeth.

Reluctantly, her aunt and uncle stood. "Well, if that's the best you can do..." Selma murmured. She glanced at Jonah in desperate appeal. "It's just a small thing we're asking."

Jonah gained his feet and gathered up the coats and scarves tossed over the back of a nearby chair. "I'll see what I can do," he whispered as he helped Selma on with hers.

"Such a good boy," she said, giving him a delighted smile. "So reasonable. And by the way, welcome to the family."

"Why, thank you." He shook hands once again with Ernie. "I'm sure Nikki will be in touch soon."

"Excellent, excellent," Ernie replied in a hearty voice as he pulled on his gloves. "Took one look and knew you were the man to make her see reason."

"Uncle Ernie—" Nikki began.

"Now, now." He enveloped her in a fierce bear hug. "Don't be too hard on yourself, Nikki. You do your best. But it's clear this husband of yours knows a thing or two about finances. Can't hurt to have him take a look at Tucker's prospectus.''

With a final goodbye, the two left. Jonah glanced at Nikki. She stood with her back to him, her vibrant hair restrained by a wide gold clip. She'd changed out of her office clothes. Gone was the stark gray suit from that morning and in its place she'd donned ivory slacks and an oversize cable sweater in a jewel-bright emerald. He could feel the tension emanating from her and stood unmoving, anticipating the explosion. He didn't have long to wait.

"How dare you?" she demanded as she swung around. She stalked toward him, her eyes blazing with amethyst fire. "How dare you interfere in a family matter?"

"I *am* family." He smiled blandly. "Or have you forgotten?"

She halted a few feet away. "I wish I could forget," she informed him passionately, tossing her notepad and pen onto the glass-topped coffee table. "But you make that impossible."

"Good. Impossible works for me."

He watched her frustration gather, watched the struggle to control her temper. And watched her fail. "Why are you butting in where you don't belong?"

"In case you weren't aware of the fact, that marriage license you were so hot to acquire came with a few strings. I'm family now, whether you like it or not. Family is allowed to butt in." He closed the distance between them, towering over her. He didn't care if she found his size intimidating. He hoped he intimidated the hell out of her. "And as long as I'm your husband, you'll treat me with the proper respect that entails. Is that clear?"

"And if I don't?"

"You don't want to know the answer to that." He thrust a hand through his hair and glared at her from beneath drawn brows, allowing a small measure of his own anger to show. "You allowed me to walk into that situation blind tonight. Do you have any idea how that felt? I didn't have a clue who those people were. Selma may not have realized, but Ernie sure as hell did. Nor have you bothered to inform me of their invitations, something else he picked up on."

She managed to meet his gaze this time, but a hint of her earlier chagrin still lingered. "I didn't think you'd be interested," she claimed.

"Don't lie to me, Nikki," he snapped. "I won't tolerate it. That's not the reason and you damned well know it. You wanted to keep me well away from your aunt and uncle."

"With good reason."

"Oh? And just what is that good reason?"

She folded her arms across her chest in a defensive gesture. "Our marriage isn't real. That's why."

He shrugged. "What difference does that make?"

She gave him an impatient look. "You know what difference. I don't want them to count on your being there when we both know it won't last. In case you didn't notice, they're a sweet couple whose affections are easily engaged."

"Mmm. I did notice," he admitted, remembering Selma's instant acceptance of him.

"Exactly. They're very trusting." She scowled at him. "Too much so."

"And I'm someone they shouldn't trust?"

To his amusement, she didn't give him a straight-forward answer. "Let's just say the jury's still out," she muttered. "But that doesn't change the fact that you're returning to London soon. By the time you do, they'll have become overly fond of you. They'll also assume you've deserted me and be hurt and upset on my behalf."

"And what about you?" he questioned curiously. "Will you be hurt and upset, too?"

"Not a bit," she stated with an interesting lack of conviction. "It'll be a relief to have you gone so I can get my life back to normal."

"Does that mean you'll move in with Krista and Keli again?"

"Absolutely not. I still have hopes of salvaging that situation, despite your interference. Which is another reason I neglected to introduce you to my relatives. You stuck your nose in where it didn't belong with Krista. I wasn't about to have you do the same with Uncle Ernie and Aunt Selma."

"I told you why I interfered in your business with Krista."

"You didn't have all the facts then, just as you didn't tonight. You had no right to tell Ernie and Selma I'd allow them to invest that money until you had all the information at your disposal."

"I agree."

"I—" She blinked in surprise. "What did you say?"

"You heard me. I spoke without thinking."

"Since you're being so agreeable, would you mind explaining why you jumped in?"

"Because I thought you were being unreasonable."

"*Unreasonable*? A fat lot you know!"

"Nikki…" He yanked irritably at his tie as he searched for an approach that wouldn't rouse her anger again. He shook his head at the irony. For such a cool, logical female, she sure had a hot temper. "They're your relatives, not your clients. Maybe if you stopped treating them as if it was a business transaction and started treating them like family—"

"I'm responsible for their financial stability."

"Maybe you shouldn't be."

"You don't understand."

"You know, I'm getting really tired of hearing that phrase." He shot her a penetrating look. "How can I understand when you won't explain? And don't tell me it isn't any of my business, because as of now I'm making it my business."

She lifted her chin. "And if I refuse to tell you anything?"

"I suspect your relatives will be more forthcoming. Of course, it might be somewhat embarrassing for you when I get my answers from them—answers my wife should have provided."

Agitation brought renewed color to her cheeks. "That's blackmail."

He tilted his head to one side in mock contemplation. "I believe you're right. It is."

"Why are you doing this?" she demanded in frustration. "What do you care? They're not your relatives."

He shrugged. "Damned if I know. I guess because I take my family obligations seriously."

"Then—"

"Enough, Nikki. Are you going to answer my questions or do I have a man-to-man conversation with Ernie?"

Stubborn to the end, she stewed about it for a full two minutes. Since he considered the outcome inevitable, he gave her all the time she needed. He crossed to the liquor cabinet and removed a bottle of cabernet sauvignon. By the time he'd poured them each a glass, she'd reached her decision. He waited while she gathered her composure, understanding her dilemma better than she realized. To discuss family, she had to give up a certain amount of control and trust him. And for some reason—perhaps that incident seven years ago—control was everything to her; trust something to be avoided at all costs.

"Well?" he asked, handing her the wine.

She took a disrespectful gulp and fixed him with a defiant glare. "What do you want to know?"

"How old was Krista when she married?"

Nikki dropped onto the couch. "Seventeen," she said bleakly.

He had suspected as much, but it still came as a shock. "She was pregnant with Keli?"

"Yes, though it wasn't a shotgun marriage, if that's what you're asking. She and Benjie were very much in love. Krista gave birth two days before her eighteenth birthday."

"That makes Keli, what? Six?" At Nikki's nod of confirmation, he asked, "And what happened to Benjie?"

"He died in a car accident four months after the wedding."

Jonah sucked in his breath. "Jeez, Nikki. I'm sorry."

"We all were," she said with marked understatement. "It wasn't a good time."

"I'll bet. What did Krista do?"

Nikki shrugged, staring into the ruby depths of her wine. "Benjie's family wasn't in a financial position to help, whereas our parents had left us some insurance money. So, Krista moved in with me."

"And has lived with you ever since," he concluded. "You've supported them?"

"Krista has a part-time job. But I've encouraged her to stay at home with Keli. I earn enough to take care of them."

"What happened to change all that? Have you gotten tired of living in such tight quarters? Or is having a six-year-old around cramping your life-style?"

She set the glass on the coffee table with great care before turning on him with all the ferocity of a tigress defending her young. "Don't you ever say that again," she said harshly. "Ever. I love Krista and have adored Keli from the moment of her birth. If I had my preference, they'd never leave."

"Then why the hell are you throwing them out?"

Emotions chased across her expressive face—pain, sorrow, resignation. "I finally realized that Krista was using me to hide from life. She never dates, rarely goes out with friends. Her entire life revolves around Keli, and to a lesser extent, me. I overheard a phone conversation shortly before the Cinderella Ball. She was explaining to a friend how much she owed me, how she could never leave me because I needed her. And I realized that all these years..." Nikki snatched up her glass and drained the contents.

Without a word, Jonah refilled it. "All these years you've protected her from life instead of forcing her to face up to it."

"Yes."

"So you've decided to set her free. In fact, you're tossing her out of the nest whether she wants to go or not."

She nodded, tears glittering on the ends of her lashes. "I've come home every day for the past six years to a hug from Keli, and now... And now—" Her voice broke and she buried her face in her hands.

He was beside her in an instant, gathering her in his arms. "Don't," he murmured. "I'm sorry. You're right. I did misunderstand."

"Keli should have a father. And Krista should have a husband." She visibly fought for control, but a stray tear escaped unchecked. "But as long as I'm in the picture, that won't happen."

"What about you?" he asked quietly, rubbing her back in slow, gentle circles. "You say that Krista's subconsciously used you as a shield, protecting herself from further pain. But haven't you been doing the same?"

She stilled. "What are you talking about?"

"I don't think Krista was the only one hurt seven years ago. Selma implied—"

"My aunt talks too much."

"There was a man, though. Wasn't there?"

"You don't under—"

He stopped the words with his mouth, tired of hearing them. She tasted of wine, the flavor far sweeter than anything he'd ever poured from a bottle. It would be all too easy to lose himself in the pleasure of the moment. But that had to wait. Right now he needed answers. "Don't lie to me again. Not now," he muttered against her lips. "Was there a man? Yes or no."

"Yes."

He cupped her chin, forcing her to meet his gaze. Her mouth was pink and damp from his kiss and distracting as hell. "What happened? Did he desert you because of Krista?"

Her breath escaped in a harsh laugh. "You're way off."

"But you loved him and he left you."

"Oh, yes. He left."

"And for the past six or seven years you've remained as cloistered as Krista."

"I've been pursuing my career," she retorted, stung. "Not living in a convent."

He slid his hand down the length of her neck to the fragile bones beneath the neckline of her sweater. "Really? And how many men have there been since the one who deserted you?" She attempted to pull free, but he tightened his hold, refusing to release her. "How many, Nikki? One? Two? Or none?"

"None," she whispered, the fight draining from her.

"Because they all threatened to take something from you," he persisted. "They wanted pieces of you that you weren't willing to give."

"Isn't that what love is all about?" she asked cynically. "Giving up control to another person?"

"Is that how it is with Krista and Keli?"

"That's different," she denied instantly. "They're family."

"How is it different? You give pieces of yourself to them," he pointed out.

The tears had returned and she stared at him, her eyes glimmering with jewel-like brilliance. "But they don't use up those pieces," she whispered. "They cherish them, make them more complete rather than less."

He'd never heard a more poignant description, a description that mated the ultimate joy love could bring with the devastating possibility of betrayal. Unable to resist any longer, he drew her close. Employing infinite tenderness, he captured her tremulous mouth with his, probing the moist warmth within.

The man who'd betrayed her had been a fool, Jonah decided in that instant. To have all this and use it so cavalierly was a crime. He might not have loved her, but he didn't have to destroy her in the process.

Jonah removed the clip confining her hair and lowered her to the couch cushions. It had been weeks since he'd had the opportunity to run his hands through the silken strands. He'd found that he wanted to do it at the oddest times—when they'd sat across each other at the dinner table, when he'd come into her office unexpectedly and caught her twirling a lock of hair around her finger. Even in the midst of one of their arguments, the temptation had struck. But not once had he given in. Until now.

Her deep russet hair spilled through his hands and across the white couch cushions, fire on ice. She was the most beautiful woman he'd ever seen. And as he held her in his arms, she responded so passionately to his kisses that her beauty took on a sensual wildness he found fiercely arousing.

"Jonah," she whispered, tugging at the buttons of his shirt. "Let me touch you."

He helped, yanking off his tie and ripping his shirt free of his trousers. Then he turned his attention to her, sliding his hands beneath the bottom of her sweater and along an endless expanse of baby-soft skin. Nothing hindered his progress, not even the expected scrap of lace and silk. With a husky moan, he cupped her breasts, his thumbs scraping across the sensitive crowns. The breath burst from her in frantic gasps and he drank in every minute sound.

But it wasn't enough. He wanted more of her.

Reluctantly releasing her mouth, he swept the bulky sweater over her head and tossed it aside. She froze beneath him, the chilly air momentarily bringing her to full awareness. He hesitated, reluctant to push her any further, ready to back off if she took fright. But far from panicking, she shivered at his touch, her spine arching reflexively.

"They're even softer than I remember," he commented, filling his hands with the abundance of wealth.

To his amusement, his twenty-eight-year-old wife blushed. "I thought your memories of that night were hazy."

"Not all of them. Of course, I was too tired to take advantage of my position then." He met her eyes with a determination she couldn't mistake. "But I'm not tonight."

Her eyes took on the most intense violet glow he'd ever seen and his gut clenched in reaction. He wanted her. Desperately. With a fierceness he hadn't felt with any other woman. The knowledge came as a distinct shock. He'd been aware of a nagging desire for weeks now. But he'd assumed it was a simple physical urge that would be satisfied with the inevitable bedding. After all, she was beautiful enough to attract any man worthy of the name. But this went deeper.

Curiosity ate at him, a need to see if she was as soft as he remembered, if her skin was as white, her legs as long and shapely. Like having a craving that demanded satisfaction, he found he had to explore the womanly secrets hidden beneath her clothing or go quietly insane.

He didn't just want to possess her body.

He wanted to lose himself in all of her—mind, body and spirit.

As a result, he'd pressed her hard tonight, forcing the issues she'd been using as a shield. Well, he'd stripped her of most of that armor and been pleasantly surprised by what she'd been hiding. Far from the cold, calculating creature he'd anticipated, he'd found a warm, generous woman, willing to sacrifice her own happiness for a member of her family.

She felt incredibly delicate beneath him, fragile and breakable. He took his time, warming her cool skin with his hands and mouth, lighting a fire that would burn bright enough to engulf them both. When she rewarded his patience with the sweetest of responses, he peeled away her slacks, uncovering legs that seemed to go on forever. He palmed the spot where delicate ankles met trim calves, and her eyes drifted closed, a soft sigh melting off her lips. His fingers danced higher, over her knee to the enticing curve of her thigh, pausing at the wisp of white that concealed russet-masked secrets. His breath grew harsh with need.

His control wouldn't last much longer, he realized, sparing her a brief glance. What he saw stopped him cold. Her violet-blue gaze met his with such a mix of need and anxiety, it threatened to unman him. And suddenly he knew he'd be making a terrible mistake if he didn't stop. Reluctantly, his hand slid away. "I won't take advantage of you like this. I'm not that other man."

"I know you're not," she whispered.

"I don't want any regrets come morning and if I'm not mistaken you already look like a woman with regrets."

She moistened her lips with the tip of her tongue. "No, really. It's all right."

But the anxiety remained and he saw it. "Well, it's not all right with me." He couldn't reach her sweater, so snagged his shirt instead, wrapping it around her. It didn't cover her completely, but it helped cool the fire to a manageable level. He pulled the collar tight beneath her chin and leveled her with a direct look. "In case you weren't aware of it, my sweet wife, making love—not having sex, but making love—means giving up a certain amount of control. But it's control freely given by both parties.''

"I know that," she began.

"No. I don't think you do. I suspect you were forced to give everything while your partner took everything. I gather some men prefer it that way. I'm not one of them. I want the woman I'm with to be a full participant. And I won't take anything I'm not also willing to give. Until you realize that and trust me, I'll pass, thanks."

"Trust you," she repeated. Her bleak laugh was heartbreaking. "You don't ask for much, do you?"

He didn't answer, just kept looking at her with those calm, hazel eyes. She struggled upright, curling her legs beneath her. It was so tempting to tell him everything— about the Miracle Box, about her parents' deaths and the aftermath. It was especially tempting to tell him about that other humiliating incident.

But he was a temporary addition to her life and she an "accidental" wife, a choice he'd reluctantly made and within hours regretted. She couldn't depend on him. She couldn't depend on anyone but herself. She'd learned that lesson the hard way and spent the past seven years making certain she didn't repeat it. She'd also spent those years compensating for that one single blunder.

Still, for the first time, she wanted someone. Needed someone. The urge to trust trembled within, like a bird desperately seeking to escape confinement. "Jonah—"

"Don't force it, sweetheart," he said gently. "I'm not going anywhere."

"Not yet," she responded bitterly.

"Not yet," he confirmed. "Go to bed. We'll talk more in the morning."

"Maybe by then I'll have come to my senses," she muttered.

He merely grinned. "I couldn't be that lucky."

CHAPTER EIGHT

NIKKI awoke the next morning to discover Jonah waiting for her at the breakfast table. Over the past few weeks they'd been careful to time their comings and goings to avoid each other. Apparently, last night had changed all that.

He filled two earthenware mugs with coffee, added sugar to each and set them side by side in front of her. To her relief, he didn't say a word until she'd consumed the first cup. Then he poured some for himself, replaced her empty mug with a platter of toasted English muffins and joined her at the table.

"Don't think me ungrateful, but what brought on this sudden burst of domesticity?" she questioned cautiously, helping herself to a muffin. "Or don't I want to know?"

"You probably don't want to know."

"But you're going to tell me anyway, right?"

"Yes." He leaned back in the chair and folded his arms across his chest. The movement pulled his crisp white shirt taut across the generous spread of his shoulders. She had vivid memories of those shoulders in all their naked glory. Too vivid. "We neglected to discuss Ernie and Selma's dilemma last night," he reminded her.

"Mmm. We did get distracted, didn't we?" she murmured, burying her nose in her coffee mug so she wouldn't get distracted again this morning.

"Pleasantly so, I hope."

138

She didn't dare answer that one, not when she caught a glimpse of green flame smoldering deep within his gaze. "What did you want to know?" she asked, hoping to move the conversation into safer channels. It would seem that talking about family now qualified as a safe topic. The irony of that fact didn't escape her.

A brief smile of awareness touched his mouth. "I want to know everything, of course. We can start, however, with your role as financial advisor. How did that come about?"

"I inherited it," she explained with a shrug. "My father was the family accountant. When he died, everyone turned to me because I was majoring in finance at the time."

He took a swallow of coffee and studied her with a thoughtful air. "You were a bit young to take on such a burden, don't you think?"

Privately, she was in complete agreement. Aloud she said, "They didn't trust anyone else."

"Ah. That old issue of trust rears its ugly head."

"Can we move this along?" she asked, reaching for another muffin to hide behind.

She wanted to get off the subject of the past. Badly. And since the future was just as uncomfortable a topic, that left the present. To her secret disgust, the idea of telling him about the Miracle Box actually held some appeal. Quite a change from how she'd felt before last night. If she wasn't careful, she really would start to trust him.

"I still have one or two questions about the past," he said, a hint of steel appearing beneath the congenial surface. "Your aunt made a reference to an incident that happened six or seven years ago and involved you. What was that about?"

"It wouldn't interest you," she replied with deceptive calm. "What's the problem, Jonah?" she couldn't resist taunting. "I thought you'd want all the gory details of how I'm being a coldhearted Scrooge and refusing to give my relatives their money. Instead, you're obsessing about a chapter of my life that's over and forgotten ages ago."

He didn't take the bait as she'd hoped. "Over, perhaps. But not forgotten." He allowed an uncomfortable silence to descend before adding, "You're not going to be able to duck a discussion of the past forever. You realize that, don't you?"

"I don't realize that at all." She fixed him with a determined look. "What I am willing to do is explain my current actions since they're of such importance to you. But my past and my future can't be of any interest."

He simply smiled. "You'd be amazed at what interests me."

Flustered, she made a production of dumping another spoonful of sugar into her coffee. "There's no point in getting too involved with each other's lives. Ours is a temporary arrangement, remember?"

"All too well." He leaned forward and caught her hand before she could spoon any more sugar into her mug. "I'll make you a deal. You stay out of the sugar bowl and I'll stay out of your past."

"Deal," she agreed instantly.

Amusement gleamed in his eyes. "At least I'll stay out for now. In the meantime, tell me about this investment."

"Right. The investment." Wriggling her fingers free of his hold, she stood and crossed to the sink, adding more coffee to her cup to dilute the abundance of sugar. "My dear aunt and uncle have been offered the unbelievable chance to own the exclusive local franchise on something called a Miracle Box."

"Never heard of it."

"Really?" she drawled in exaggerated surprise. "But it's a brilliant invention. Absolutely everyone is going to want one."

"What does this Miracle Box do?" he asked warily.

"Let's see if I can remember it all...." Turning to face him, she leaned against the counter and took a quick sip of coffee. She fought to hide her grimace of distaste. It needed more sugar again, but she'd cut off her hand before reaching for that bowl. "It's part fax/modem, part telephone answering machine and part cable TV receiver and VCR all in one convenient, plug-into-the-wall device."

"And I'll bet it washes dishes and gives change for a dollar, too," Jonah said drily.

"Not yet. But only because the inventor hasn't thought of it." She frowned. "The problem is that this Miracle Box sounds just close enough to what's already on the market or soon to be available that to people like Ernie or Selma it appears quite believable."

"Interesting scam."

She gave a short laugh. "Oh, but I haven't told you the best part yet."

"Well? Don't keep me in suspense. What's the best part?"

"My aunt and uncle can have this exclusive franchise for the rock-bottom price of fifty grand."

She'd stunned him with that one. "You're kidding."

"I'm dead serious. Not only has he conned them into believing this box will make them a fortune, but he's buffaloed my cousins, as well. Which means that everyone will be so busy selling the Miracle Box, they'll neglect Ernie's Beanery."

Jonah shook his head in disgust. "By the time they realize it's all a scam, business will have bottomed out."

"And my family will be under investigation for fraud. If neglect doesn't succeed in destroying their café, lawyers' fees certainly will. But the bottom line will be the same. They will have happily paid fifty thousand dollars to put Ernie's Beanery out of business and themselves into bankruptcy."

"I'm sorry, Nikki. I should have—"

She cocked an eyebrow. "Trusted me?"

"Something like that," he conceded.

"That's all right. I have a bit of trouble in that department, too." She dumped the remains of her coffee in the sink and rinsed the mug. "Well, I'll tell you how you can make it up to me...."

"You want me to tell them they can't have the money," he said in a resigned voice.

She hid a smile. "Why, thank you. I accept. Shall we go into work now or shall I introduce you to the Beanery?"

"You say that as if I have a choice."

"The Beanery it is." She didn't bother to hide her grin. "Tell you what. I'll let *you* do the talking this time."

Jan opened the office door and poked her head in. "Sorry to disturb you, Nikki."

Nikki shoved aside the papers she'd been working on and glanced at her secretary. "What's up?"

"There's a man on line two who insists on speaking to you. He won't leave his name or number and this is the third time he's called. Do you want to talk to him or should I try to find out who it is again?"

Nikki shook her head. "No, don't bother. I'll take it, thanks." She reached for the phone and punched the appropriate button. "Nikki Alexander," she stated automatically. She'd certainly grown accustomed to using her married name, she realized with a bittersweet smile. She'd better hope she found it just as easy to get *un*used to.

"Ah, Mrs. Alexander. At last. You're a very difficult woman to get hold of."

"Who is this, please?"

"Timothy T. Tucker. I'm sure you've heard of me."

Nikki straightened in her chair. "I don't believe it. Mr. Miracle Box himself."

"The one and only. I spoke to your aunt and uncle this morning and there seems to be a small problem."

"Oh?" she drawled. "And what might that be?"

"Ernie's having trouble getting his hands on the money to invest in my proposition."

"And he gave you my number?"

There was a small pause. "Several of them," he said deliberately.

Her eyes narrowed. What did that mean? Had Uncle Ernie been foolish enough to supply this man with her number at Jonah's apartment? She stirred uneasily. And what about the brownstone? The idea of Tucker having Krista's number was very unsettling. "What do you want?" she demanded.

"I want the money Ernie and Selma promised me. Fifty thousand to be exact."

"I'm sorry, Mr. Tucker. Perhaps my aunt and uncle neglected to mention it. They've chosen not to invest in your scam—" she deliberately paused before correcting herself "—I mean, in your invention."

"I don't think you understand—"

"No, it's you who doesn't understand," she informed him crisply. "My aunt and uncle may be gullible, but I'm not. I've examined your prospectus and plan to hand it over to the appropriate authorities."

"What the hell are you talking about?"

She swiveled in her chair to face the office window. "I'm talking about fraud. The technology you claim to have doesn't exist."

"My box—"

"Your box is as phony as you are. Goodbye, Mr. Tucker."

"I wouldn't hang up if I were you! You better give your uncle that money, or you'll regret it."

"I don't think so."

"Oh, no? Your aunt and uncle aren't just gullible. They're also very talkative. And I'm a great listener. In all my conversations with them, they were quite full of their brilliant niece." His deliberate pause was an exact copy of her own. "Brilliant *now*, that is."

She slowly straightened. "Get to the point, Tucker."

"You weren't quite so brilliant seven years ago, were you? I think the LJB committee would be very interested in the details of that little escapade, don't you?"

Her hand tightened on the receiver. "Are you threatening me?"

"Oh, no. I'm making you a one hundred percent guarantee. You ruin my deal with your aunt and uncle, and I expose that nasty little skeleton in your closet. Look at it as an investment in your own personal Miracle Box. Fifty grand in exchange for a box that does absolutely nothing. You have my personal guarantee that it won't make so much as a peep." He laughed raucously at his own joke. "So, is it a deal?"

Nikki closed her eyes. All she'd worked for over the past seven years, all she'd done to try to make up for that one horrible disaster would be for nothing. She knew the interpretation people would put on that incident. Not only would the award committee take away her nomination, she'd undoubtedly lose her job, as well. But to pay this slime fifty thousand in the hopes that he wouldn't say anything?

"Not a chance," she whispered. "I don't pay blackmail. Do your worst, Tucker."

"I plan to," he snarled and slammed down the phone.

Nikki hung up, staring blindly out the window. So what did she do now? Without conscious thought, she crossed to the office closet and pulled out her box of gardening supplies. For the next hour, she worked and weighed her options. Briefly, she considered going to Jonah for help. It was possible he'd understand. After all, he'd understood about Krista. He'd also understood about her aunt and uncle. He'd even gone to them and explained that Tucker was a con man, all the while handling the situation with a diplomacy she couldn't have emulated on her best day.

Then he'd taken his assistance one step further. He'd supported her advice that they use their savings to open a second Ernie's Beanery and employ her cousins to run it. By the time he'd walked out of the café, they'd all fallen in love with him.

Just as she had.

The breath stopped in her throat and she closed her eyes, fighting the sudden and inescapable knowledge. No. She couldn't be that irresponsible. She couldn't truly love him. Love was for fools. Love forced a person to give up control. Love didn't work for her; she'd resigned herself to that fact. But she'd never lied to herself before and didn't intend to start now. Slowly, carefully, she searched her heart. And there she saw the truth.

She didn't know when or how it had happened. Perhaps it had come on her bit by bit without her even being aware. Still, that didn't change the fundamental truth. She did love him, with a bone-deep intensity. Where once she thought her heart and soul irreparably damaged, now she saw they'd been healed. And that healing was due to one man.

Jonah.

But to have fallen in love. She shook her head. How foolish of her. Because if she loved him, that meant she trusted him. And if she trusted him, she'd have to tell him about...

Tucker.

She shuddered. She couldn't dump this on Jonah, couldn't watch the green fire in his gaze turn to gold ice. Perhaps if he loved her in return, she'd take the risk of telling him about the past. But the painful fact of the matter was...he didn't love her. Oh, he wanted her. And he'd make sure she found their time together special, no matter how brief. But in the end, he'd leave and she'd be alone once again.

Which still left the main question unanswered.

What did she do now?

Nothing, she decided at last. She couldn't be certain that Tucker would make good on his threat. By doing so, he risked exposing himself. And slime like that preferred operating in the safety of the shadows. Too much light brought too much attention.

A peremptory knock sounded at her office door. "Nikki? I wanted to talk to you about—" Jonah stepped across the threshold and stopped dead, staring at her in astonishment. "What the hell are you doing?"

"Potting plants," she replied with a self-conscious shrug. "Or rather, repotting. I do it whenever I need to think."

His narrowed gaze swung to the empty windowsill and back again. "So, you weren't killing them. You were saving them."

She glared at him indignantly and started to put her hands on her hips. Just in time, she remembered she still wore her gardening gloves. "You thought I was killing plants?" she demanded, stripping off the gloves and tossing them to the protective tarp. "On purpose?"

"You'll have to forgive my ignorance," he said gently. "At the time I came to that conclusion, I didn't know what a maternal soul you had."

His assessment gave her an odd feeling. She'd never considered herself the least maternal. She was a career woman first and foremost. Any fleeting thoughts she might have indulged with regard to children had been just that. Fleeting. Besides, she had Keli. She bit her lip. *Had* being the operative word. Soon she wouldn't even have that, not if her plan succeeded.

"What are you thinking?"

She avoided his gaze. "Nothing important." Removing her apron, she began loading her supplies into the box.

"You were thinking about Keli, weren't you?"

His perception dismayed her. "Yes," she admitted, aware that denials were pointless.

"Haven't you ever considered marrying?" He edged his hip onto the corner of her desk, his trousers pulled taut across his thighs. "For real, I mean? Having children of your own?"

"Once."

"Ah. Seven years ago again. We really must clear the air about that."

"Did I mention? I'm beginning to like coffee unsweetened." She shoved the box in the direction of the closet, hoping that would close the subject. "I assume you came in here for some reason other than to annoy me."

"Not really." His large hands closed around her waist and he lifted her aside. "Allow me." With an ease she could only envy, he hoisted the box as though it were weightless and deposited it in the closet.

"Thanks," she murmured.

"No problem." Turning, he scrutinized her with unnerving intensity. Almost hesitantly, he reached out and swept a stray lock of hair from her temple. Then with a muffled exclamation, he thrust his hands deep into her topknot. Her hair came loose, spilling in heavy waves about her face. "Temptress," he muttered, drawing her close.

"Jonah—"

But his mouth stopped her incipient protest. And then it stopped all thought. It had become easier and easier to give in to him—especially when his demands so closely matched her own desires. She wrapped her arms around him, not the least surprised when he crushed her along his hard length, tugging her between his legs and against the very heart of him.

"Am I interrupting something?" an amused voice asked from the doorway. They both spun around. Eric stood there, leaning against the jamb. "You took so long getting that update on the Dearfield account," he addressed Jonah, "that I decided to come looking for you."

Jonah swore beneath his breath. "Right. The Dearfield account."

Hot color swept across Nikki's cheekbones. "I have the update with my files. Let me get it for you."

"I guess the honeymoon's not over yet, huh?" Eric asked innocently.

Nikki stared at him in horror, unable to say a word.

"What the hell does that mean?" Jonah growled, shooting her an uneasy glance. "We're not on our honeymoon."

Eric shrugged. "That's not what it looks like to me."

"You—you're wrong," Nikki managed to say.

"Of course I am." He stepped into the room, grinning. "Good thing I'm not a client, though. Not very professional, you know, making love on the office floor. Or were you planning on using the desk?"

"Go to hell, little brother," Jonah snapped. "The day I need a lecture from you about professionalism—"

Eric held up his hands. "Okay, okay. Though at least allow me to suggest you lock the door next time."

Jonah's hands balled into fists. "Why you—"

"Stop it!" To Nikki's horror, tears pricked her eyes. Stress. It had to be stress. Between her family problems, her marriage and Tucker, it was a wonder she hadn't gone completely insane. "Here's the update," she said, tossing the file onto her desk. "Now, if you'll excuse me?" She didn't give either man a chance to reply, but swept from the room before she disgraced herself completely.

Jonah started to follow, but Eric caught his arm. "She won't thank you for going after her. Women prefer to conduct these crying jags in private."

"What! She was crying?"

Eric shrugged. "I thought I caught a glimpse of tears."

"Damn." A resigned expression crossed Jonah's face. "Mind telling me what makes you such an expert all of the sudden?"

"Just using a little common sense for a change. And as long as I'm so full of it, so to speak, I'll offer you some more advice. Give her time." He paused a beat. "The first year of marriage can be tough on a couple."

"And I told you this isn't—"

"It's as good as. You can't count *your* first year. You didn't spend any of it together," Eric argued reasonably.

"I...she..."

"Yes?"

"Forget it!"

Eric slanted him a sly look. "Your wife sure was upset."

Jonah's gaze followed the direction Nikki had taken. "Bad, huh?"

"Has to be stress," Eric pronounced thoughtfully as he headed for the door. He glanced over his shoulder. "I mean, it can't be sexual tension. Now can it? Not after what I just saw." The door quietly closing punctuated his observation.

"It can't be sexual tension. Now can it?"

In the three days since Eric had made the comment, Jonah had been consumed by that thought to the exclusion of all else. *Sexual tension.* He pushed his fork around his dinner plate, cursing beneath his breath. Oh, he was tense all right. Very tense. Very, very tense and getting tenser by the minute. He scowled across the table at his wife. Not that she noticed.

Nikki stared at her plate, struggling to work up sufficient enthusiasm to eat. For the past three days, she'd been consumed with thoughts of her husband, and of love and trust and horrible men who made horrible threats. She'd also spent the time trying to decide how to handle the predicament she'd gotten herself into. In fact, it had become a daily battle—whether or not to trust the man she loved, despite the fact that he didn't love her. She peeked at Jonah from beneath her lashes. Not that he noticed.

Jonah threw down his fork. If his brother were here now, he'd strangle the smart-mouthed little—

"What did you say?" Nikki asked.

"I said, I've had enough."

"I'm sorry. Don't you like it?" She glanced down at her own plate of linguini. "Too rich, huh?"

"Actually, I've changed my mind. I haven't had enough." He shoved back his chair. "But I'm about to change that. Right now."

She tilted her head to one side, the candlelight catching in the ruby tones of her hair. "You want seconds?"

"No. I want firsts."

Her brows drew together in delicious bewilderment. "I don't understand."

"You will." He circled the table, and without further ado, lifted her into his arms. "Catching on yet?"

"Jonah! What—what are you doing?"

"What I *would* have done that first night if I hadn't been so tired. What I *should* have done three nights ago, if I hadn't gotten so involved in playing the noble husband." The bedroom door blocked his path and he kicked it open. "And what I'm *going* to do right now because it's what we've both wanted from the instant we met."

He tossed her onto the mattress, waiting for the inevitable argument.

She didn't say a word.

He waited for anxiety to turn her eyes the color of amethysts. They slowly changed color, but it was passion that lurked in the violet depths, not fear.

He waited for her to flee. Instead, she remained in the middle of the bed.

Her very inaction sealed her fate. He approached, unable to take his eyes from her. Her skin gleamed like ivory, while her hair was a vivid splash of darkest crimson against the black down comforter. His gaze never left her as he ripped off his shirt. His shoes came next, then his belt. Finally, he reached for the zip on his pants. Her eyes grew huge and the tip of her tongue appeared, skating across her bottom lip.

He wanted that lip, he decided. He wanted it for an appetizer. He wanted to nibble on it, to sink his teeth into its fullness before exploring within. And once he'd temporarily sated himself with her mouth, he wanted to taste his way downward, sampling every inch of her, course after delicious course. It would be the most magnificent feast he'd ever consumed. And for dessert, he'd return to the sweetness of her mouth.

"To hell with linguini," he muttered, settling onto the bed beside her. "Nothing can be more satisfying than this."

Nikki stared at him in utter astonishment. After three full days of endless confusion and doubt, it took a split second to realize the undeniable truth. Not only did she love Jonah, she trusted him. Totally. Implicitly. Without reservation. And with that knowledge came the most amazing sense of freedom. Joy welled within. She could tell him. She could tell him everything and he'd understand.

He gathered her close, resting half on top of her, his hands sinking into her hair. "Speak now, wife," he muttered, catching her lower lip between his teeth. "Or forever hold your peace."

"I'd rather hold you," she whispered. Wrapping her arms around his neck, she returned the passion of his kiss. Tomorrow they would talk. But right now, there were more important matters to take care of. They had the give and take of their latest merger to work out.

Removing her clothing became a serious negotiation. The zipper of her skirt voiced a loud argument as he drew it downward. Each button of her blouse needed to be coaxed free of its hole. Her lacy garters had to be convinced to release their tight embrace on her silk stockings. And the hooks and eyes of her bra had to be rescued from their enforced closure. But she found that having a brilliant negotiator for a husband had certain advantages. With due patience and diligence, he overcame every dilemma.

And the end result was the most satisfying she'd ever known.

She lay within the safe circle of his arms, coming alive beneath his touch, on fire for him and for him alone. And she discovered the unassailable truth of his earlier observations. Making love *was* a partnership. For everything she gave him, she received tenfold in return. The more she opened to him, the more he opened to her. To offer a delicate kiss had him returning it with a deeper one. Slipping her hands across the endless expanse of his chest led to his painting lazy circles around the rosy tips of her breasts. And when she shyly initiated a more intimate caress, he unlocked passionate secrets that had been trapped within her for years, giving her a pleasure she'd never before experienced.

"Do you trust me?" he demanded at one point.

Tears welled into her eyes and she visibly fought to control them. "I—I haven't dared to," she admitted in a broken voice. Slowly, she looked at him. "Until now."

He cradled her close. "Are you sure? Very sure?"

"Yes," she whispered. "I'm positive."

And with her words still lingering between them, he mated his body with hers, taking her with exquisite care and tenderness. It was as though he sealed her pledge of trust with his body and offered her love's ultimate completion as his return promise. Without fear or hesitation, without thought to what the morrow might bring, she gave herself to him. She gave all of herself, holding nothing back, discovering the full height and depth of love.

And when ecstasy finally came, it was within the sheltering embrace of her husband, the one man she'd love to the end of time.

Nikki lay quietly as dawn lit up the sky with the promise of a new day. And in that moment of earth's gradual awakening, she listened to her inner voice, waiting for the doubt and uncertainty to return. But nothing disturbed the smooth tenor of her thoughts. She felt now as she had last night. If there was one man in the world she could trust, it was Jonah.

Rolling onto her side to face him, she discovered him already awake and watching her with an unnerving intensity. "Good morning," she whispered.

"Waking up with you in my bed is nice," he murmured in a sleep-husky voice. "The only thing better would be waking up with you in my arms."

She smiled and snuggled closer, happy to accommodate. He punched the pillows behind him, shifting to recline against them. She nestled her head into the crook of his shoulder and threaded her fingers through the thick mat of hair covering his powerful chest. His heart beat slow and steady beneath her palm.

Gently, he cupped the side of her face with his large hand, his thumb stroking across her cheekbone. She leaned into the tender caress.

It was time for the truth.

"Jonah?"

"I'm here, sweetheart."

She took a deep breath, awed at the ease with which the words came. "I need your help."

His thumb never stopped its calm, soothing motion, but the tiny tremor that shook his hand told her a very different emotion raged within. "How can I help?" he asked with gruff simplicity.

CHAPTER NINE

"NIKKI? Are you home?" Jonah crushed the paper in his fist, frustrated anger darkening his eyes. "Sweetheart?"

"I'm here."

She appeared in the doorway to the bedroom, dressed in a black silk slip and damned little else. If it had been any other time, he'd have snatched her into his arms and returned to the bedroom with her. There he'd have removed that bit of nothing and made love to her until they were both too exhausted to move, think or even speak. Especially speak. As it was, he brushed past her, grabbed a thick terry robe and held it out.

"Put this on. We need to talk."

A warm smile tugged at her full, kissable mouth, tempting him almost beyond endurance. "I can't talk to you wearing my slip?" she teased.

"It depends on the kind of talking you want to get done."

He tucked the newspaper beneath his arm and helped her on with the robe. Jerking the front closed over the plunging black neckline, his knuckles scraped over her full breasts and he stilled, caught between desperate desire and the need to give her the bad news. As much as he'd like to delay the inevitable, they had too much to accomplish if they were to avert disaster.

Sweeping her hair from beneath the collar of her robe, he gathered a handful of the silken tresses in his fist and contented himself with a prolonged kiss. Just like every other time he touched her, she melted into his arms, her lush curves settling against him in a way guaranteed to send his blood pressure through the roof. And just like every other time he touched her, she gave totally of herself, never holding anything back. Reluctantly, he ended the embrace.

She blinked up at him. Her eyes—as soft and velvety as pansies—expressed absolute faith and confidence. He stifled a groan. Heaven help him. When his wife decided to trust him, she didn't bother with half measures. It was all or nothing.

He wrapped an arm around her and headed for the kitchen. "Let's fix some coffee."

She lifted an eyebrow, a hint of concern creeping into her expression. "Coffee or something stronger?"

"I'd prefer something stronger. But we'll stick with coffee." Moving with brisk efficiency, he dumped ground beans into the filter, added the water and hit the start button. "You can even have sugar with it."

"So the worst has happened," she murmured.

"Yeah, it happened." He dropped the newspaper onto the tile counter. It was one of the more disreputable rags floating around the city. "LJB Award Nominee Swindled Family Out Of Inheritance!" the headline screamed.

She squared her shoulders and faced him. "Am I fired?"

"How can you even ask such a question?" he snapped.

"You have to protect International Investment. I understand that." She responded with such cool logic, he wanted to grab hold and kiss her until her teeth rattled. Or until she regained her senses.

He shoved his hands into his pockets to quell the impulse, settling for an unsatisfactory glare of annoyance to express his irritation. "International Investment will ride out this particular storm just fine without any noble gestures on your part.''

She set her rounded chin at a stubborn angle. ''I'll tender my resignation effective immediately,'' she said as though he hadn't spoken. ''And as soon as I've dressed, I'll go in and clear out my desk.''

''Stop it, Nikki.''

''No, it's all right. I knew this could happen when I refused to submit to Tucker's blackmail scheme.''

''Refusing to have any further dealings with that man was one of the few intelligent decisions you've made since we met. And before you ask, the other was confiding in me.''

''It's not your problem,'' she insisted. ''I'll handle it.''

''You asked for my help the other night, remember? I told you then I'd deal with Tucker.''

She bowed her head. ''I know you did your best.''

He bit back an exclamation of fury. She was determined to play the tragic martyr and he knew of only one way to snap her out of it. ''What happened to all that talk of trust?'' he questioned caustically. ''Or was that all it was—just talk?''

As he hoped, her head jerked up, her eyes flashing with violet fire. ''It wasn't just talk!''

''Then trust me, damn it. I'll stop that piece of slime if it's the last thing I do.''

''But what about in the meantime? How long can you protect me if International Investment starts losing customers? What are you going to say to your clients? Yes, she swindled her relatives, but she won't do it to you?''

''You didn't swindle anyone!'' he roared.

The momentary silence was deafening. Then the coffee machine gave a final, inelegant burp and she offered a watery laugh. ''Thank you for your support.''

"My pleasure." He filled three mugs, automatically setting two in front of Nikki. Shooting her an assessing glance, he wondered how best to break the next bit of news. "Sweetheart..."

She kept her gaze fixed on the sugar, determinedly spooning it into her mugs. "There's more, isn't there?"

He sighed. "I'm afraid so."

She took a fortifying gulp of coffee. "Tell me the rest."

"The LJB nomination committee has requested that you attend a special session to determine whether you should be dropped as a candidate."

"When?"

"Nine, Monday morning."

"Three days." She caught her lip between her teeth. "Who brought the charges? Or is that a ridiculous question?"

"They refused to say. But I think we both know who's responsible."

A fine line appeared between her drawn brows. "I can't do this, Jonah. I can't go before those people and talk about my past. It was difficult enough telling you." He could see the panic she fought so hard to suppress. "They're strangers. They'll never understand."

"We'll make them understand."

She stilled. "We?"

"I'll be right there beside you."

He'd surprised her with that one. Hope dawned in her eyes. "You're going?"

"You're my wife. Of course I'm going. I wouldn't let you deal with this alone."

Words eluded her. She shoved her coffee aside and covered her face with her hands.

He slammed his mug to the counter and pulled her to her feet, catching her in a rib-cracking embrace. "I have it on excellent authority that women prefer conducting these crying jags in private," he murmured against the silky top of her head. "But I refuse to leave you alone right now. So I'm afraid you're stuck with me."

"I don't want to be left alone," she responded in a muffled voice. "Please hold me."

"I'm not going anywhere," he assured her.

"Yet."

His mouth compressed at the reminder. They'd both been careful to avoid a discussion of the future and he had no intention of correcting that oversight. At least, not now. "That's right," he said at last. "I'm not going anywhere. Yet."

"Jonah," she whispered, "I'm afraid."

He swung her up into his arms, cradling her close. Her head drooped against his shoulder like a delicate rose with a damaged stem. She felt so fragile, so vulnerable. The instinctive urge to protect gripped him— the unshakable need to defend her from harm. And like a feral animal determined to keep his mate safe, he strode toward the sanctuary of his lair.

Monday arrived all too soon as far as Nikki was concerned. Choosing an outfit to wear before the committee—or "inquisitors" as Jonah insisted on dubbing them—became a major undertaking. The minute she plucked a garment from the closet, Jonah categorically rejected it.

"Too depressing," he pronounced, tossing aside the severe black suit she'd selected. "Besides, it makes you look guilty."

"What do you want me to wear?" she demanded in exasperation. "My wedding outfit? That's about all I have left."

"It's a thought. Wait a sec. Aha." He yanked a stylish ivory suit and matching silk blouse from the closet. "Here we go. This, gold jewelry and heels."

She stared at him in disbelief. "You're not serious, are you? Jonah, this isn't a business suit. I bought it to wear last Easter."

"Exactly. I want them to take one look at you and think, 'innocent'. And this outfit will do it."

"In case you've forgotten, I *am* innocent," she muttered.

He turned, the look on his face instantly silencing her. "I haven't forgotten a thing. And once the LJB committee has seen and heard you, they won't have any doubts, either." He handed her the suit. "Put this on. Oh, and leave your hair down."

"Anything else?"

"Yeah." His eyes blazed with suggestive green highlights. "Make sure you wear silk and lace underwear, stockings with those sexy little seams in the back, and garters."

She planted her hands on her hips. "That's supposed to make the committee think I'm innocent?"

"No." He dropped a swift, hard kiss on her mouth. "The silk and lace is for me. The committee will just have to sit there and wonder what you have on under all that soft lamb's wool. But I'll know."

A reluctant smile tugged at her lips. "You're impossible." She found it incredible that she could find anything humorous at a time like this. Thanks to her husband, she had. She peeked up at him. He never ceased to amaze her.

"It'll be our little secret," he said, rubbing his hands together. "Anytime I start to lose my temper, I'll think of popping those flimsy little garters. It'll wreak havoc with my self-control, but it should keep me from blowing a fuse.''

"Great. And what am I supposed to think about?''

He leaned down, nestling his mouth close to her ear. "You think about what I'm wearing under my suit.''

Her eyes gleamed with laughter. "You have something hidden in there I don't know about?''

"Could be...'' His grin was wickedly sensual. "But I'm not telling. You'll just have to find out for yourself after the meeting.''

"You're going to make me wait that long? No fair!'' she protested.

"Ah, but there's method to my madness. Anytime you feel panicky, I want you to think about what it might be.''

"And that's supposed to calm me?'' He couldn't know how he affected her if he thought that. She couldn't look at him, touch him, listen to the deep, rough tones of his voice without a desperate need sweeping through her.

"If nothing else, it should distract you.'' He gave her a gentle swat on her backside. "Get dressed, wife. I'll fix breakfast.''

"One cup of coffee this morning,'' she requested. At his questioning look, she added, "I'm jittery enough without the extra caffeine.''

"Beauty combined with intelligence. We can't lose.''

His comment helped her get through breakfast and the cab ride to the office complex where the nomination committee had scheduled the meeting. The first attack of butterflies didn't hit until they entered the elevator. To her surprise, Jonah must have felt something similar. Ignoring their fellow passengers, he reached out and captured her hand.

"White?'' he asked.

She stared in bewilderment. "What?"

"The garters. Are they white?"

She blushed at the amused sidelong looks they received. "Ivory," she whispered. "With pink rosebuds."

He closed his eyes and grinned. "Oh, yeah."

She peeked over at him. "Boxers?"

"Not telling."

A picture of Jonah leaping into bed in a pair of Santa-festooned shorts flashed through her mind and she fought to suppress a giggle.

The elevator door opened just then, and squeezing her hand, Jonah forged a path from the back of the car. "We're on," he warned. "Be confident. We're in the right here."

"Okay." As they approached the reception area, she asked softly, "Bikini briefs?"

"Nope."

"May I help you?" the receptionist said with a congenial smile.

"Mr. and Mrs. Alexander to see the nomination committee."

"Yes, you're expected. Follow me, please." She led the way down a short hallway and paused to knock on a set of double doors.

A sudden thought occurred to Nikki and she caught Jonah's hand before he could walk into the conference room. "Wait! You do have on...? You're not totally...?" She couldn't say it, her gaze drifting downward in fascinated horror.

"Oh, no?" He gave her a slow wink, then thrust the doors open, stepping boldly across the threshold. "What do you say we get this show on the road?" he demanded.

Two women and three men were grouped at one end of the room. At Nikki and Jonah's entrance, the five swiveled in unison, like puppets on a string. A tall, gruff-looking man built on proportions similar to Jonah took the initiative and approached.

"Bill West. I'm the committee chairman," he said, shaking hands with each of them, before turning his attention back to Jonah. "We didn't expect to see you this morning, Mr. Alexander."

"No, I'm sure you didn't. But I'm here nonetheless." He cocked an eyebrow. "I trust you have no objections?"

"Would it matter if I did?"

"No."

A reluctant smile creased Bill's mouth. "I didn't think so," he murmured drily. "Well, you're welcome to observe. But you do understand that the accusations have been leveled against your wife and the answers will have to come from her."

"What I realize is that we're here at your request to answer unsubstantiated allegations. We're doing it as a courtesy and without benefit of counsel. Should, in the course of this...*meeting*, I feel that situation should change, I'll inform you." His wintry gaze held Bill's for a long moment. "*Now* I believe we understand each other. Do you agree?"

"Oh, yes. We understand each other perfectly." The chairman gestured toward the conference table. "Make yourself comfortable. Can I get you anything? Water, coffee?"

"Three coffees. Two with sugar, one plain," Jonah ordered briskly. Turning, he escorted Nikki to the far end of the table, then held the chair for her.

"I didn't want any coffee," she whispered as she took her seat.

"I know. I just did it to tick him off. It's a power thing."

"Thanks," she said wryly. "I'm sure that 'power thing' will help the inquisition go much smoother." She folded her hands demurely in her lap. "By the way, did I mention that I have precisely five items on under my suit?"

She slanted a quick peek at him from beneath her lashes. As she'd anticipated, he was conducting a rapid-fire inventory and coming up precisely one item short. She smothered a smile. Jonah wasn't the only one capable of pulling a "power thing". Wondering what she'd left off should keep him busy for a while. At least she hoped it would.

"Your coffee," Bill announced heartily, as an underling scurried in, setting cups and saucers in front of them. "Now. Shall we begin?"

"You ready, Nikki?" Jonah asked.

"As ready as I'll ever be."

Bill joined the other four members at the opposite end of the table. "First let me say, Mrs. Alexander, that we apologize for the inconvenience." A deep frown creased his brow. "Unfortunately, it's important we clear this business up. Lawrence J. Bauman nominees must be above reproach. Companies who hire our candidates demand it. Why, a nomination alone can assure a position at the most select firms."

"I already have a position at one of the most select firms," Nikki inserted smoothly.

Jonah smiled in appreciation at her comment. "And the select firm in question supports Mrs. Alexander fully in this matter."

Bill sighed. "Yes, Mr. Alexander. We're well aware of your support. We're also well aware of International

Investment's standing in the business world. Nevertheless, due to the seriousness of the charges, we're forced to investigate this matter to the fullest. We don't like it. You don't like it. But we have no choice if we're to survive public scrutiny.''

''What would you like to know?'' Nikki asked, taking a sip of coffee and struggling to hide a grimace at the lack of sugar. Without missing a beat, Jonah switched cups with her.

''I have information here from an unnamed individual—''

''Timothy T. Tucker,'' she interjected again.

''You know this man?''

''Yes. He attempted to sell my aunt and uncle his...invention. When I recommended against it, he threatened to publicize details of my past.''

''Tell them the rest,'' Jonah prompted.

She didn't question his directive, but simply said, ''Tucker also offered to keep quiet if I changed my recommendation and authorized payment to him to the tune of fifty thousand dollars.''

The committee paused for a moment's discussion. Then Bill nodded. ''We suspected that Mr. Tucker's motives for providing this information were questionable at best. But that's beside the point. What we must ascertain is whether the information is accurate.''

''You'll have to be more specific,'' Jonah requested crisply.

''Very well. Let's get into specifics.'' Bill consulted his notes before fixing Nikki with his undivided attention. ''Did you take money belonging to your relatives and invest it in worthless real estate?''

''One moment, please,'' Jonah interrupted. He leaned close, gathering her hands in his. ''Give them the honest truth," he instructed calmly, his thumb tracing the outline of her wedding band. "Don't hesitate in answering. Don't attempt to explain at this point. They don't want explanations, just an admission."

Her fingers tightened on his. "And you want me to give them that admission?" The butterflies in her stomach had become a swarm of hornets.

"I want you to give it to them." He met her eyes unflinchingly, the utter confidence in his gaze easing her fears. How could she have ever thought those eyes resembled the bitter chill of autumn? she wondered in confusion. She must have been blind. They exactly matched the brilliant greens and golds of a warm spring day. "Trust me," he said.

"You know I do." She glanced at Bill West and flushed. "I'm sorry. Would you please repeat the question?"

He released an impatient sigh. "Did you take money belonging to your relatives and invest it in worthless real estate?"

She didn't look at Jonah. She didn't need to. "Yes," she said.

Her answer clearly surprised him. He referred to his notes again. "And did you then borrow money from the bank in order to finance an additional purchase?"

"I did."

The questions came faster. "And did you lose that money?"

"Yes."

"Did the bank foreclose on the original property when you were unable to make the monthly payments?"

"They did."

"And did the lending institute discover that the appraisal had been fraudulently obtained and that the property wasn't worth anything close to what you'd borrowed against it?''

"It was worth approximately half of what I'd borrowed," she confessed.

Bill tossed down his pen and stared in dismay. "Mrs. Alexander, I'm at a loss for words. These are very serious charges and you've admitted to each and every one of them."

"Yes, Mr. West, I'm well aware of that. But these questions were asked out of context. I assume you'll permit me to put them in context?"

"If you can," Bill retorted.

She spared Jonah a brief glance. He gave her an encouraging nod, and drawing a deep breath, she began to explain. "Eight years ago, my parents died—"

The woman on Bill's left stirred, the overhead lights picking out the iron gray streaks in her hair. "I hardly see what the death of your parents has to do with these proceedings—"

"My wife has extended you the courtesy of listening and responding to each of your allegations," Jonah cut in, his fury barely held in check. "You'll do no less for her."

"He's right, Clara. Let her tell the story her way. It's the least we can do," Bill said reasonably. "We apologize, Mrs. Alexander. Please continue."

"Their deaths have quite a lot to do with this story," Nikki responded. "I'm sure you'll understand that it precipitated a major crisis in my family. Not only did we suffer from the emotional loss, but my mother and father were also the financial advisers for a number of my relatives. Because I was studying business at the time of their deaths, that burden then fell to me." A self-mocking smile flitted across her mouth. "Youth combined with an unfortunate arrogance allowed me to think I could handle the responsibility."

"I suspect we've all been there at one point or another," Bill murmured.

"I'm relieved to hear it. In my case, I had a college professor who'd become my mentor and encouraged me in my new capacity. Whenever I had a question, he'd advise me. About the time I turned twenty-one, he left the university to pursue more lucrative opportunities."

"Real-estate investment?" Bill guessed shrewdly.

"The very real-estate investment for which I'm currently under investigation," she confirmed.

Jonah spoke up again. "I'd like to make it clear— since I doubt my wife will—that at this point in her life she was also supporting a pregnant younger sister who'd just been widowed. Although Nikki's parents had left some insurance money, I question that it was sufficient to cover the expenses she was incurring at that time."

"No, it wasn't," Nikki admitted. "I suppose that's why I was vulnerable to Professor Wyman's offer."

"Professor Wyman?" Clara interrupted again. "Professor Wilbert Wyman?"

"Yes. Although he preferred people to call him Bert." Nikki looked at her curiously. "Do you know him?"

"My—my daughter did." Her hand clenched around her pen. "I'm sorry. Please go on."

"Bert showed me a commercial property that he felt would be a guaranteed money-maker. Funny... I still remember the name. Sunrise Center. Anyway, he was incredibly enthusiastic, said that if I didn't grab it, he would." She shrugged. "So I grabbed it."

"You went to your relatives for the money?"

She nodded. "We used everything we had—my parents' insurance money, my aunt and uncle's nest egg . . ." Her voice grew husky with remorse. "Even the funds set aside for my cousins' college tuition."

"Didn't you consider that risky?"

It took a minute to gather the emotional resilience to respond. "Not a day goes by that I don't regret having taken that risk," she told them with devastating candor. "But you can't make money without risking money. Or so Bert said."

"What happened then?"

The words came more easily. "Once I'd finalized the purchase, he came to me with a second proposal. He wanted me to borrow money from the bank against the property I'd just bought."

"What did he want you to do with that money?"

"He suggested we invest it in what he called a short-term turnaround. We'd buy and sell this surefire money-maker within the space of a few months." She played with her coffee cup, remembering the naive fool she'd been. She started to pick up the cup, but her hands shook so badly, she returned it to the saucer. "I should have known it was too good to be true. Later, I learned that Bert had bribed the appraiser to grossly inflate the value of Sunrise Center. As a result, the bank loaned me over twice its value."

"And the money?"

"I handed the check over to Bert." She tried to smile. "Quite the brilliant young finance student, wasn't I?"

"I assume Bert promptly disappeared with the funds?" Bill questioned gently.

"Yes."

"What in the world did you do?"

She gathered the last of her inner resources, struggling to summarize the most difficult time of her life with as little emotion as possible. "I spent the next seven years working harder than I ever had before. I learned everything I could about the business world so I'd never be taken like that again. And I gradually paid back the money to the bank, to my aunt and uncle, to my cousins and to my sister. With interest. Last year, thanks to several legitimate investments, I was able to square all accounts."

"And what happened to Professor Wyman?"

"I have no idea. I assume he went on to scam other gullible college students."

"He did," Clara inserted softly. "But not for long. He was sent to prison five years ago."

Nikki stared at her, stunned.

Without further ado, Bill gathered his notes. "Thank you, Mrs. Alexander. That will be all."

"No, that damned well won't be all," Jonah bit out. "We'll hear your results here and now. Is she still a nominee or do I contact my lawyers?"

"Don't, Jonah," Nikki whispered, slipping icy fingers into the welcoming warmth of his huge hand. "And just so you know....I'm wearing two stockings, one garter, a slip and one more item."

She'd managed to distract him. "Which did you leave off?" he demanded softly. "Top or bottom?"

"You figure it out." She raised her voice. "I don't intend to contest your decision. But in all fairness, I do think I deserve an expeditious finding."

"One moment please." There was a hushed conference among the committee. "We have no objection to giving you an immediate ruling. Assuming we find no discrepancy in the statement you've given, your nomination will stand."

"And how long will it take to look for any discrepancies?" Jonah questioned irascibly.

"The ceremony is Saturday. If Mrs. Alexander's status changes, you'll be notified by Friday."

Afraid of what Jonah might say to that, Nikki stood. "Thank you for the opportunity to answer your questions." She tucked her hand into the crook of Jonah's arm and, using every ounce of her strength, dragged him from the room. "You are more stubborn than any mule," she muttered.

His hand coasted down her spine before settling in the small of her back. Abruptly, he stopped fighting. "Come on. Let's go home," he said.

"What's the sudden hurry?" she asked, eyeing him suspiciously.

He stabbed the button for the elevator. "I think I know what that missing item is."

She lifted an eyebrow. "Oh?"

"Yeah." He grinned, tugging her into the empty car. "If I'm right, it's the same item I'm missing. And I've decided I'd much rather find out for sure than argue with a bunch of stuffy committee members."

"Me, too." She snuggled into the crook of his arm, sliding an experimental hand along his hip. "Good grief, Jonah! You really aren't—"

The elevator door banged closed.

CHAPTER TEN

"Aren't you nervous?" Selma questioned.

"Well, I—"

"Why should she be nervous?" Krista said dismissively. "She's a shoo-in."

Nikki gave a self-conscious shrug. "Oh, I doubt—"

"Damn that Tucker anyway." Ernie glared across the width of the huge stretch limo. "Why didn't you tell us about him, Nikki? I'd have strangled the little weasel when I had the chance."

"But I did—"

"Thank heaven for Jonah," Selma inserted, offering him a dazzling smile of unabashed approval. "I don't know what we would have done without his guidance."

"Yes. Thank heaven I was there," he agreed, draping an arm around Nikki's shoulders. "After all, it's a husband's duty and moral obligation to protect his wife."

"And the little woman's family, too?" she finally erupted.

"Yes, that, too." His grin flashed in the darkness. "Feel better now?"

She nodded, the momentary anger siphoning off some of her tension. "Much."

"Good." His eyes glinted from the shadows as he shifted closer. "Have I mentioned how beautiful you look tonight, Mrs. Alexander?" he asked, nuzzling the spot just beneath her left ear.

"Hey, hey! None of that," Eric protested. "You can celebrate after she's won."

"*If* I win," she hastened to correct. "Which is doubtful. I hope all of you won't be too disappointed."

"No one's going to be disappointed," Jonah said as the limo pulled up in front of the hotel. He peered out the window. "Good. They're here."

Nikki strained to see past his bulky shoulders. "Who? Who's here?"

"Mom and Dad," Eric replied. "They decided to catch a cab directly from the hotel instead of taking the limo with us."

"I think I'm going to be ill," Nikki said with a groan. "You didn't warn me they'd be coming."

"They're here to support you, just like we are." Jonah caught her fingers in his, squeezing gently. "Ivory?" he whispered.

She sighed, relaxing against him. "Black. Boxers?"

"Thong."

A watery laugh shivered between them. "Don't tease."

"Who's teasing?"

The door opened, ending any further conversation. Loren and Della hurried forward to greet her with effusive hugs and kisses, acting as though she truly was their daughter-in-law. And she found herself wishing it was fact and not just a momentary fantasy. Once inside the hotel, they were directed to a huge, glittering ballroom where a table had been reserved for them close to the stage. Other nominees graced nearby tables. Dinner and speeches followed, dragging out the evening. By the time Bill West took the stage carrying the LJB Award, Nikki's nerves were stretched taut.

"Before I make the big announcement," he began, "I'd like to tell you a little about the winner of this year's Lawrence J. Bauman Award. The person we've selected epitomizes the standards for which the award was designed—brilliance, dedication, shrewd business acumen and, above all else, integrity. This individual possesses those qualities and a few more besides. It was those extra few qualities that allowed our committee to reach an immediate and unanimous decision.''

''That's you, dear. It has to be,'' Selma whispered.

Tears gathered in Nikki's eyes and wordlessly she shook her head. The moment he'd used the word ''integrity'', she'd known they'd chosen someone else. Not that it came as any great surprise.

''This person has surmounted terrible adversity,'' Bill continued, ''not just learning from and overcoming past mistakes, but benefiting from them, as well. No mountain proved too high, no problem slipped by until an honorable solution had been found, no moral dilemma went without the appropriate choice being made, no matter how difficult that choice might be. So, without further ado, it is my great honor and privilege to present this year's Lawrence J. Bauman Award to... Mrs. Nikki Ashton Alexander.''

Nikki was so shocked, she couldn't move for a full minute. Jonah came to her rescue, sweeping her from the chair and into his arms. Giving her a hard kiss, he aimed her toward the stage. ''You earned it, sweetheart. Now go get it.''

She weaved through the tables, climbing the steps to the podium in a total daze. Bill West shook her hand, then held out the crystal-and-gold award. Accepting it, she stared blindly at the graceful design, fighting for control. After the scandal had broken, she'd counted herself fortunate to have retained her status as a nominee. But she hadn't expected to win. She honestly hadn't. She looked up, realizing in dawning horror that she would have to make a speech. But from the moment her name had been called, her mind had gone blank.

"I—I..." Her throat closed up, her self-control deserting her. Just as panic seemed her only remaining option, her gaze fell on Jonah. It only took one look at his calm, steadying features to quiet the inner tumult. Heaven help her, but she loved that man.

Taking a deep breath, she said, "My thanks to the LJB nominating committee for both this award and the opportunity to set the record straight." She glanced at Loren and Della. "To International Investment, I extend my deepest appreciation for their unwavering support in the face of overwhelming adversity. It was more than I expected and certainly more than I deserved."

Her hands trembled and she'd have given anything to flee the stage at that point rather than bare her soul to public scrutiny. But opportunities like this only came along once in a lifetime. And she owed some people. It was time they knew it. "I'd like to thank my family for their enduring love and faith in my ability. They deserve this award far more than I. For such intelligent people, they took some foolish risks with their continued backing."

Ernie and Selma beamed. Krista just shook her head with a hint of exasperation. Nikki's gaze sought Jonah's once more. "And, finally, I want to thank my husband, Jonah." She struggled to subdue the husky catch in her voice. But she couldn't. So she just said the words, allowing the emotion to spill free. "You gave me something I thought lost to me forever. Thank you for proving it's possible to trust again. Because without trust—"

Her voice broke, destroying what little remained of her composure. The room grew hushed as everyone waited to see what she would do or say next. She caught

her lip between her teeth. Never had she wanted so badly
to cut and run. But she was determined to finish. Jonah
deserved no less. Gripping the award so tightly she feared
it would shatter in her hands, she spoke with heartfelt
sincerity. "Thank you for proving it's possible to trust
again. Because without trust, you can't have love."

She didn't remember much after that. Somehow she
got off the stage and back to the table. There she endured a thousand hugs and handshakes. But all she really
wanted was to walk into the protective warmth of Jonah's
arms and never leave. Unfortunately, she couldn't even
get near him. He stood off to one side, a cryptic smile
on his face, watching as she accepted the unending flood
of congratulations.

"I say we all go out and party," Krista suggested, once
the room had begun to empty. "Champagne, caviar, the
works."

Eric nodded in agreement. "After all, we do have two
reasons to celebrate. Nikki's award and..." He grinned,
holding up Krista's left hand. A huge diamond solitaire
sparkled on her ring finger. "We're engaged."

Nikki stared in astonishment, unable to move, unable
to even draw breath.

Krista giggled, snuggling against Eric. "Your expression is priceless, big sister. I guess you didn't see
that one coming."

"Now you two don't have to stay married if you'd
rather not," Eric added, his gaze moving from her to
Jonah.

Nikki's mouth fell open. "What?" she managed to
say.

"The Cinderella Ball," Krista explained. "Between
us, Eric and I figured out the truth about that night. We

also realized that you and Jonah must have married for our sakes—you know, so we'd get on with our lives.''

Eric dropped a kiss on his fiancée's cheek. ''And we have. Although I'll bet you didn't expect us to do it together.''

Nikki darted a quick look at Jonah. If his expression had been difficult to read before, now it was utterly impossible. ''I don't understand. How did you two meet?'' she asked her sister.

''I came by the office to see you,'' Krista explained. ''But you were busy. I bumped into Eric and he invited me to lunch.''

''One thing led to another,'' he said, picking up the tale. ''And here we are. So, although we appreciate what you've done you don't have to keep pretending.'' A wily grin touched his mouth. ''Unless, of course, you've fallen madly in love and want to stay married.''

''That's enough, Eric,'' Jonah cut in. He offered his hand. ''Congratulations. And I agree with your suggestion. This does deserve a celebration.'' For the first time, he turned to Nikki. ''Doesn't it? After all, you finally have everything you ever wanted. Right?''

Nikki tossed her coat onto the couch and carefully placed her award on the coffee table. ''What are we going to do?'' she asked without turning around. She was afraid to face him, afraid of what she'd read in Jonah's cool, remote gaze.

''I don't know about you, but I'm going to hit the sack,'' he replied with a shrug. ''You're welcome to join me if you'd like.''

''That's not what I meant.''

His sigh held an impatient edge. "If you're referring to our future, I don't think this is the time for that particular discussion."

Dread ran an icy finger along her spine. "Why not?"

"Because I leave for London in the morning."

"*London*?" She sank onto the couch, staring in disbelief. "You never said...you never mentioned..."

"I didn't mention it earlier," he explained evenly, "because I felt you had enough to deal with."

She laced her fingers together to hide how badly they trembled. "Your return to London...is it permanent?"

He stilled. And suddenly he seemed larger, harder, tougher. "You have to ask?"

She bowed her head. "Oh, that's right. You promised Ernie and Selma you'd be here for Christmas. I assume you intend to keep that engagement?"

"What the hell do you think?" The words sounded like they'd been torn from him. "Have I ever failed to keep a promise I've made?"

"No," she whispered. "You've kept every one. And you've done an excellent job of it, too. Thanks."

His coat hit the arm of the couch and tumbled to the floor unheeded. "I don't want your damned thanks," he said with barely restrained fury.

She lifted a hand in appeal. "Then what do you want?"

"The one thing it seems you find impossible to give, despite tonight's fine speech."

"You want my trust?" she asked in confusion. "You have it."

"Do I?" He ripped the bow tie from around his throat. "Prove it."

"How?" she demanded. "You don't have a family who needs rescuing. Your reputation isn't in jeopardy.

Neither is your job. You don't have any deep, dark skeletons in your past that I can magnanimously overlook. I have no way of proving myself.''

But she did, and she knew it. All she had to do was speak three simple words. Tell him what she'd kept so carefully hidden within her heart. Trust him with that final piece of herself. The words fought for escape, fought to wing free. But, in the end, fear kept them locked tightly away.

He stood mute and aloof, watching and waiting as she waged her inner battle.

Desperate to give him the proof he needed without having to surrender that final bit of control, she left the couch. Reaching for the side zip of her dress, she yanked it down, the black silk puddling at her ankles. She stepped over the inky pool and approached. To her dismay, he made no move to either accept or reject her overture.

''Jonah, please...'' She slid her palms along the taut muscles of his chest, wrapping her arms around his neck.

His hands closed on her shoulders. For an instant, she thought he'd push her away. Instead, he pulled her close, holding her against him for several, silent minutes. Then he thrust his fingers deep into her hair and tugged her head back, gazing down at her as though memorizing each tiny detail of her face.

''Kiss me goodbye, Nikki,'' he whispered.

Tears gathered in her eyes. ''Not goodbye,'' she insisted frantically. ''You'll return for Christmas. You promised.''

''Let's not drag this out. Kiss me, sweetheart.''

''But your flight isn't until tomorrow. We still have tonight.''

He shook his head. "I leave early in the morning, so I'll stay at one of the airport hotels for the remainder of the evening."

She moistened her lips, searching wildly for a way to delay him. "You—you still need to pack."

"I have a bag ready to go."

"This is it?" Her chin quivered. "You're just going to walk away?"

He lowered his head, the tenderness of his kiss almost destroying her. "What is there to keep me?" he asked.

He didn't wait for a response. Releasing her, he snagged his coat from off the floor. And moments later, he was gone.

Nikki awoke the next morning to a cold and empty bed. She also woke to discover that Jonah had kept his final promise. On the front page of the newspaper was an article reporting the arrest of Timothy T. Tucker for fraud. Credit for information leading to the arrest was attributed to an unnamed concerned citizen. But Nikki didn't need to question the identity of that "concerned citizen".

She knew it was Jonah.

The next several days were the most miserable of Nikki's existence. She'd thought signing the bank's money over to Bert Wyman had been the biggest mistake she'd ever made. But she soon discovered it didn't come close to equaling the one she'd made with Jonah.

The only excuse she'd been able to come up with to explain her idiocy was that she'd been caught off guard. The shock of Eric and Krista's announcement coming on the heels of her own emotion-laden win at the award ceremony had ended in sheer, unadulterated panic.

Maybe if she'd had time to calm down, she would have been all right. Just a few days in which to get used to the idea that she and Jonah had precisely one reason left for continuing their marriage.

Love.

And she did love Jonah, despite being unable to tell him. It had taken hours of soul-searching, but she'd finally concluded that it wasn't saying the actual words she'd feared most. It was his response to her declaration. She was terrified that he didn't love her in return.

Yet he'd demonstrated over and over how much he cared. He'd helped her resolve her problems with Eric and Krista. He'd rescued her family from a con man and solidified their financial well-being. He'd salvaged her reputation, standing by her in word and deed when no one else would have.

And with each and every tender touch, he'd shown the depth of his feelings.

Prove it, he'd said. Prove she trusted him.

Prove that she loved him, was what he really meant.

Suddenly, she knew the perfect way. She could say the words, but somehow she suspected that wouldn't be enough. Not any longer. She reached for the phone, wondering if she'd have sufficient time to put her plan into action. It'd take a bit of work. Arranging for the fax and the plants would be the easy part. It was the Christmas gift she intended to have delivered that might take extra effort.

But if she could just pull this off, it would be worth it in the end.

Christmas Eve ended up being the longest day of Nikki's life.

She went into the office, running on sheer nerves. She kept wondering if Jonah had received her fax, worrying that she'd waited too long before contacting him, and panicking over whether or not his special gift would arrive in time. The only thing she didn't question was her feelings for him.

Or his for her.

By early afternoon, the last of the employees had left for the holidays. The building grew silent and vacant and vaguely cold. Reluctant to return to an apartment empty of Jonah's dynamic presence, she stood in the darkness staring out the window at the bustling crowd. A bittersweet smile touched her mouth. They were all rushing to get home, to share in the warmth and joy of the season. How she wanted that, too!

As she watched, the first flakes of snow tumbled through the inky night sky. Keli would be thrilled. She'd have a white Christmas. Nikki closed her eyes, desperately fighting to hold the tears at bay. But would all that beautiful snow delay Jonah?

She wanted him. Heaven help her, she needed his strength and tenderness and love. Why hadn't she just told him the truth when she'd had the chance? How could she have risked losing the single most important person in her life? She bowed her head, her breath catching on a sob.

Please, she prayed, *just let him get home safely*. It didn't matter if he was late. It didn't matter if his present didn't arrive on time. Nothing mattered, except that he return to her whole and healthy.

Behind her, something hit her desk with a soft thud. She spun around with a gasp. A file lay spotlighted in the middle of the oak surface—a file that hadn't been there moments before. Hardly daring to breathe, she crept closer, struggling to read the name through her tears.

It was the Stamberg account.

From the darkness, a shirt came flying through the air. Then a tie. And then a belt.

"Jonah," she cried, torn between laughing and giving in to her tears. "What are you doing?"

"Making good on our bet, of course."

She covered her mouth with her hand. Angels singing heavenly hymns couldn't have equaled the beautiful sound made by Jonah's rough, husky voice. "You're going to dance naked on my desk?" she demanded.

"Unless you have a better place for me to dance naked."

Laughter won out. "I have a much better place." Impatience lent wings to her feet and she raced around the desk, hurling herself against the wide, comforting breadth of him. "Did you get my fax?"

"I got it. And I must say, it caused quite a stir at the office." He tilted his head to one side. "Let's see ... how did it read?"

"'Jonah, please come home. Urgent. There's something I forgot to tell you,'" Nikki quoted softly.

"Everyone thinks you're pregnant." He snagged her chin in his huge hand. "You're not, are you?"

"No." A minute frown crept between her brows. "At least, I don't think so."

"Too bad. It would have simplified matters."

She rubbed her cheek against his palm. "I'm not very good at simple," she confided. "Somehow I always end up doing it the hard way."

"I've noticed," he said with unmistakable tenderness. "So what did you forget to tell me?"

She took a deep breath. "I forgot to tell you that I love you. In fact, I forgot to tell you that I love you very, very much."

A slow smile touched his mouth. From there, it expanded into his eyes, the autumn chill melting into a rich spring warmth. "I'm supposed to take your word for that?"

"Yes. Because—" she glanced swiftly at him from beneath her lashes "—I think you love me, too."

He cocked an eyebrow. "You think?"

"I know," she corrected hastily. "I know you love me. And I thought of a way to prove my feelings for you."

He was openly grinning now. "And how's that, Mrs. Alexander?"

"Well..." She tightened her hold on his neck, reveling in the delicious scent and sound and touch of him. "You'll have to wait until tomorrow. But I have a few ideas that should tide you over in the meantime."

"Do any of those ideas involve getting out of the rest of our clothes?"

She laughed. "At least one of them does. But maybe you'd rather wait until we get home."

He heaved a deep sigh. "Haven't you figured it out yet? With you in my arms, I am home." His voice deepened, filled with a rich certainty, an unquestionable commitment to the future. "And by the way, my sweet wife, I love you, too. Very, very much."

And then he kissed her, proving beyond a doubt that Christmas was still a time of miracles.

When Christmas morning arrived, it proved to be the most joyous Nikki had ever experienced. Waking up in

Jonah's arms, then to his hungry kiss and finally to his urgent lovemaking got the day off to a perfect start.

Once they reluctantly left the bedroom, she showed him the changes she'd made to the apartment. Plants filled every nook and cranny. And occupying one entire corner stood a live, potted evergreen covered in lights and ornaments.

"It wouldn't be a real home without your plants," he observed quietly.

"No," she disagreed, slipping into his arms. "It wouldn't be a real home without you. The plants are just to prove that I'm here to stay."

The relatives started arriving midmorning, adding their laughter to the apartment, along with an assortment of flavorful dishes. Nikki was on tenterhooks from the moment the doorbell first rang, rushing to peek into the hallway each time she thought she heard footsteps approaching.

"Who are you expecting?" Krista asked curiously at one point. "I thought everyone was already here."

"They are—"

A knock sounded at the door just then, and breaking off, she raced to answer it. Flinging it open, she called to Jonah, "It's for you. Hurry!"

He didn't come quickly enough to suit her and she rushed to his side. Grabbing his arm, she tugged impatiently. Curious, the rest of the family followed, gathering in a loose semicircle behind him. In the hallway stood a messenger dressed in the same white-and-gold uniform that the footmen at the Cinderella Ball had worn.

"I understood this was urgent," the messenger said with a broad grin. He handed Jonah a beautifully wrapped package. "Merry Christmas."

"Open it," Nikki urged the instant they'd closed the door.

With an indulgent smile, he ripped off the bright gold paper to expose a small rectangular box. He removed the lid and looked inside. Nervously, she awaited his reaction, his expressionless face worrying her. At long last, he looked up. Ignoring the eager questions from all the relatives, he closed the box. Catching hold of her hand, he towed her through the living room and out onto the balcony.

It was freezing cold, but she barely noticed. "Jonah?" she questioned anxiously. "Don't you like it?"

He dug a hand into his pocket and pulled out a small square package. "Maybe you should see what I bought you."

She ripped off the ribbon and wrapping paper and slowly flipped open the red velvet lid. Inside nestled a pair of wedding bands. Very unique, strangely etched wedding bands. "Oh, Jonah," she whispered, tears pricking her eyes. "They're made from the tickets to the Cinderella Ball."

"It was odd. The Montagues said we're the second couple requesting rings like these."

She shook her head helplessly. "It's a beautiful idea. Thank you."

"I thought it was time we had real rings and couldn't think of anything more fitting." For the first time, a hint of uncertainty crept into his voice. "I didn't want there to be any question as to my feelings for you."

"That's why..." She gestured to the box she'd had delivered to him, fighting to speak through her tears.

Huge, puffy snowflakes began to swirl downward, catching in her hair and on the ends of her lashes. He gathered her into his arms. "That's why you gave me tickets to the Anniversary Ball."

She nodded. "It's where it all began. It's where I fell in love with you. And where I first began to trust again."

He kissed the snowflakes from her lips. "I'll never give you reason to question that trust, Nikki. I swear it."

A smile slipped across her mouth and blazed with violet certainty within her eyes. "I believe you."

And peeking through the sliding glass door at them, their entire family cheered.

*   *   *   *   *

Look out next month for Shotgun Marriage,
*the third book in Day Leclaire's
wonderful new trilogy.*

Harlequin Romance ®

SIMPLY THE BEST

Authors you'll treasure, books you'll want to keep!

Harlequin Romance books just keep getting better and better...and we're delighted to welcome you to our Simply the Best showcase for 1997.

Each month for a whole year we'll be highlighting a particular author—one we know you're going to love!

The year gets off to a great start with:

#3439 MARRIAGE BAIT
by Eva Rutland

Sparks fly when Lisa decides she isn't interested in a career—she wants a husband! Preferably a rich, glamorous one...and she'll do anything to catch one!

Available in January wherever Harlequin books are sold.

ℋarlequin Romance®

Coming Next Month

#3439 MARRIAGE BAIT Eva Rutland—Simply the Best

Lisa should have been delighted when Scott Harding offered her a dream promotion—it was the opportunity of a lifetime. But Lisa wasn't interested in a career: she wanted a husband!

Welcome to the first book in our Simply the Best showcase. Harlequin Romance books just keep getting better, and now for a whole year we'll be highlighting a particular author each month—one we know you're going to love!

#3440 SHOTGUN MARRIAGE Day Leclaire—Fairytale Weddings—#3

Harlequin Romance invites you to a wedding...

...And it could be your own!

On one very special night, single people from all over America come together in the hope of finding that special ingredient for a happy-ever-after—their soul mate. The inspiration behind the Cinderella Ball is simple—come single, leave wed. Which is exactly what happens to three unsuspecting couples in Day Leclaire's great new trilogy....

Rafe Beaumont holds the Montague family, founders of the Cinderella Ball, responsible for ruining his sister's life. Marrying Ella Montague is his way of getting revenge and proving once and for all that happy-ever-afters are strictly for fairy tales. Ella knows better—love can overcome all obstacles, even a stubborn husband!

#3441 RUNAWAY HONEYMOON Ruth Jean Dale

Cole Stadler has never forgotten—or forgiven—Jenny Wolf's running out on him. But it seems he still wants a relationship—on *his* terms. How can she prevent his discovering her five-year-old secret?

#3442 TWO-PARENT FAMILY Patricia Knoll—Baby Boom

Carrie McCoy knew plenty about babies, but it seemed that she didn't know much about men. She'd been jilted on the morning of her wedding. Will Calhoun had whisked her away from the mercy of town gossips. Then he let her in on his little pair of secrets. Ariana and Jacob were twins. They were three weeks old and they were adorable. All they needed was a mother.

We are proud to announce the birth of our new bouncing baby series—Baby Boom! Each month we'll be bringing you your very own bundle of joy—a cute and delightful romance by one of your favorite authors. This series is all about the true labor of love—parenthood and how to survive it! Because, as our heroes and heroines are about to discover, two's company and three (or four... or five) is a family!

Harlequin Romance ®

BABY BOOM

We are proud to announce the birth of our new bouncing baby series—Baby Boom!

Each month in 1997 we'll be bringing you your very own bundle of joy—a cute, delightful romance by one of your favorite authors. Our heroes and heroines are about to discover that two's company and three (or four…or five) is a family!

This exciting new series is all about the true labor of love…

Parenthood, and how to survive it!

Watch for:

#3442 TWO-PARENT FAMILY
by Patricia Knoll

Available in January wherever
Harlequin books are sold.

1997
Reader's Engagement Book
A calendar of important dates
and anniversaries for readers to use!

Informative and entertaining—with notable
dates and trivia highlighted throughout the year.

Handy, convenient, pocketbook size to help you
keep track of your own personal important dates.

Added bonus—contains $5.00 worth of coupons
for upcoming Harlequin and Silhouette books.
This calendar more than pays for itself!

 Available beginning in November at
your favorite retail outlet.